LET ME OUT HERE

LET ME

OUT HERE

STORIES

EMILY W. PEASE

HUB CITY PRESS
SPARTANBURG. SC

The following stories have appeared, in this or other forms, in: "Mating
Day," *Witness* (1997); "Church Retreat, 1975" won the Bevel Summers Prize
at *Shenandoah* magazine (2014); "Foods of the Bible" won the Crazyshorts!
contest at *Crazyhorse* magazine (2015); "Submission," *Alaska Quarterly Review*
(Winter/Spring 2018); "The After-Life," *Narrative* magazine "Story of the
Week" (2018).

Book Design: Kate McMullen
Cover photo: *Untitled, Girl with Snake, Rabun, GA* | Jennifer Garza-Cuen
Copyeditors: Andrew Dally, Kalee Lineberger
Printed in East Peoria, IL by Versa Press

Library of Congress Cataloging-in-Publication Data

Names: Pease, Emily W., author.
Title: Let me out here : stories / by Emily W. Pease.
Description: Spartanburg, SC : Hub City Press, [2019]
Identifiers: LCCN 2018031215 | ISBN 9781938235504 (book)
Classification: LCC PS3616.E2664 A6 2019 | DDC 813/.6--dc23
LC record available at https://lccn.loc.gov/2018031215

HUB CITY
PRESS

186 West Main St.
Spartanburg, SC 29306
1.864.577.9349
www.hubcity.org
www.twitter.com/hubcitypress

For Ed, Lilli, Mae, and Hunter
And in memory of my parents, Sis and Chuck Wheatley

CONTENTS

SUBMISSION

We were the family you wanted to avoid, dumb pilgrims stumbling along the Fiery Gizzard Trail on a mission. A mom and dad, a remnant of kids, and a baby riding in a flimsy stroller, its bald head flopping from side to side. The Coopers, that was us, we were that family. Our father stared straight ahead as he walked, flint-eyed, feeling with his left hand his sheathed bowie knife as if wild animals would attack us. Our mother, her skirt spattered with mud, her hair so long she could sit on it, said without looking back: stay together. The trail was slippery after days of rain. Jagged, pointy rocks, puddles, mud, fallen trees blocking our way. James, the baby's father, lifted the stroller over tree trunks, over the biggest stones, while Dundee just lay there, floppy and silent. Lacking normal muscle tone, so the doctor said.

And it was a doctor, any doctor, we Coopers were determined to avoid. Just as we avoided schools, churches, fluoride, the

I.R.S., computers, and neighborhoods. The only reason Dundee had even seen a doctor was because of his size at birth: tiny. Very, very tiny. Pencil-width arms, head no bigger than a peach. Screechy cry, a weak suck. Carlotta, age sixteen, the baby's terrified mother, my oldest sister, paced before the NICU window with her head down, not willing to look upon her red, scrawny newborn on the other side of the glass with a needle in his arm and squares of gauze hiding his eyes. All that baby needs is to be at home, our mother said. Home, surrounded by love. Her blind faith.

The doctor diagnosed hypotonia. Don't ask me how I remember this—I pretty much remember everything I hear. Hypotonia: lack of muscle tone. Probable cause: Rh incompatibility, Carlotta and James being the incompatible ones, their opposite blood types a problem even prayer couldn't fix. Yet there she was in front of me on the trail, pregnant again, on a mission to heal Dundee. As well as the baby to come. And did this new baby also belong to James, and did they still have the same incompatible blood types? Well, yes. And did they go to a doctor this time to take the necessary shots or precautions or whatever? They said they had. Even our father, who decided long ago that the medical profession is nothing but a scam, doctors being liable to give you the wrong medicines or even, as happened to his brother, operate on the wrong leg, said James and Carlotta ought to go see about the Rh factor and do whatever the doctor said. That this new baby might be strong. That this new baby might not cry with a screech in his voice and go limp in your arms when you picked him up.

Dundee. Named for the most hard-muscled man Carlotta and James could picture at the time. But a name alone won't alter a person. Or cure a person. What could cure, our family believed, was ritual: dance, smoke, prayer. Carlotta trudged ahead of me, undaunted by the trickiness of the trail. She was convinced that by hiking as a family, soft shafts of sunlight falling on our shoulders, we were already summoning spirits. She turned to me and smiled as if to say, isn't this great, Calvin? She lifted her eyes to the filtered light, the heavy hemlocks hovering over the trail, and tried to feel their energy. In sympathy I tried to feel the energy too. I tuned my ears to birdsong, to the rustle of wind in bare branches, but then she began to hum, and the spell was lost; she sounded like she was blowing through paper on a comb. Meanwhile, James had begun to curse. On the rocky slope he struggled like a fat man, a seventeen-year-old fat father of one/ two. *Damned stroller, fucking stroller, piece of shit!* I looked to the front of our little procession to check on Chrissie, age six, her fisted hand gripping our mother's skirt. She stumbled, and one of her pink sneakers wedged between two rocks. But good brave girl, she didn't cry.

To be a Cooper you had to be a certain kind of brave. Brave enough to be shunned and to shun in return. Brave enough to be in this world but not of this world. To be a believer in the one pure and real Christ while watching for a whole host of anti-Christs at the same time. And to accept that they could arrive at any minute. Kind of the way Dundee arrived, a surprise to us all, Carlotta stepping through the back door to say she didn't know what was happening, but it looked like it might be now. Eight weeks too soon. She leaned against the door frame, teeth chattering. Chrissie ran over and hugged her leg. And then a miracle happened—our father, our big, silent father, denier of all forms of medical intervention, went and got the keys to his truck. We have to go get help, he said, his voice wavering. He took Carlotta by the arm and led her out, one of those moments you never forget.

The trail was clogged with hikers, this being the first clear day in a week, close to Easter. Some schools were already out. Behind us we could hear voices, and there were shouts through the trees. Chrissie sat fiddling with her shoe. I wanted her to hurry up. I hated groups of people, especially boys, my presumed tribe. Our father pulled out his knife. He looked like he was about to skin something. On his forearm: a bleeding heart, on his wrist: a blue crown of thorns. He bent down maybe to cut her shoelaces, and there came this funny sound. Dundee gurgling in his stroller. Gurgling like something was coming up. Carlotta began to coo at him, ignoring his throaty noises. It was as if she'd just noticed we brought him along. She kissed his cheek, and our mother ran a hand over his head the way a cat licks her young.

The hikers grew nearer. Loud, loogie-hocking, and stupid. I didn't have to see them to know what they were. My keen ears could detect the fuzzy, bottled-up sound of guitar licks leaking from somebody's earbuds. Chrissie kept wiggling her wedged shoe until it finally came loose, then she stood up. Here they came, five of them, carrying tools. They were the type of guys who see a forest as something to cut down. I saw hatchets and a machete and a bush axe. One of the guys saluted me. I looked at our father, and I knew what he was thinking. *Fools.* Once again I was glad I'd never been sent to school. We stepped off the trail, James holding the stroller against his chest to let the little gang pass. The one with the earbuds came first, and his friends followed him. They stared at us, stinking, silent.

We sat for a while to let them get some distance. Why were they carrying weapons, Chrissie wanted to know, and our father told her that's what boys do. Some boys do, I almost said, but didn't. Swine, I also wanted to say—swine do, swine carry machetes and hatchets on a trail. Swine was a word I liked. We are not, Jesus said, to throw our pearls to swine. I could buy that. Then Chrissie said, so why don't you carry a weapon, daddy? And he said, laying a hand on his knife, I don't need one. In my head I thought of course not, you don't need a weapon because you could tear those boys apart with your bare hands. I saw the rabbit hutch tucked under our back fence, our family's food supply. How many rabbits had I seen him strangle?

I was starting to get hungry. We'd driven hours to get here, all of us packed in the van with the front window open so our father could smoke. In the front seat our mother kept turning on the heat and turning it off. Dundee would whimper, and Chrissie would pull a bottle out of her enormous bag, and I'd have to watch his yellow formula going down, Dundee slowly sucking. On the radio there was Limbaugh. Limbaugh and then the Bible network and then more Limbaugh. Dundee had his bottle, burped, then slept. James and Carlotta leaned on each other looking into her phone. Amazing, they let her have a phone. We were a non-technology family all the way. But somehow, Carlotta got a phone. James, I guess. Not entirely a Cooper.

It was through the miracle of her phone that Carlotta got the idea to take Dundee to a waterfall, two miles in. A miracle, too, that our father agreed. Carlotta and James did their research: closest waterfall on a public trail = Fiery Gizzard. Swimming hole = Fiery Gizzard. And wouldn't we all swim, if only it wasn't the vernal equinox, average temperature = 55 degrees. They chose the vernal equinox because it's when the center of the sun shines exactly over the equator, and day and night become equal. A turning in the seasons, a turning toward rebirth. Even I could get excited about that idea. I pictured a black shadow passing over the sun. In Carlotta's mind, everything had to have meaning. The waterfall, the time of year, the things in her bag. She talked about positive ions, how waterfalls change the air and make it purer, while our father talked about rocks. He loved rocks, started collecting them when he was a boy. Earth's core. Geodes in our front room, a hunk of quartz by the door, little stones on the windowsills in the bedroom we shared.

Our mother said, Peter was the rock! She'd been thumbing through scriptures. And Peter was a fisherman, he was on the water. He walked on water! Look, she said, water's everywhere in the Bible, beginning with Noah. And that flood healed the whole world.

Like Jonah, I said. I was my own personal worldwide web. I said, Jonah was thrown overboard to keep the boat from sinking in a storm. By Jonah, the sailors were healed.

And Moses in the bulrushes—there was a story. You could set Dundee in a basket and float him down the river in search of a better mother. This, I did not say. But then what do you know, Carlotta brought it up herself. What if we float him on the water, she said, just like Moses? Not far, just a little ways. It could be a sign of faith.

And what if, I wanted to say but didn't, I just lay down on a pyre and let our father pull out his bowie knife to cut my throat?

So many things I never say. In my head, so many things.

I did not say, for instance, while we sat around the kitchen table that day planning a hike, that a Tennessee waterfall wasn't about to change anything in Dundee's life, or the life of this new baby in the womb, or our mother's arthritis or Chrissie's nightmares or the overall strangeness of our family, which was a sickness in itself. Neither would prayer. What had prayer really done for us so far? What happened to Dundee had happened to Dundee, period. He was born too early, just like Carlotta's very first baby, the one only I knew about, the one that never grew. The one before James came around. No prayer, no dance beside a waterfall could change that story.

Or this: what it was like for me, a ten-year-old kid who'd already seen his share of nature's cruelty, to witness our mother giving birth. To Chrissie. I stood with Carlotta in the bedroom, with its many smells and mysteries, and tried to close my eyes and ears. Our mother lifted her knees. Such noise. And then the wet hairy globe—I could see no more, so I went to watch the pot on the stove. Somebody had to keep the house from burning down.

Funny how everybody has their own way of looking at the same thing. As if we can decide what's really real. Carlotta, age eleven, saw the miracle of birth. The heavens came down, and she opened her arms. Filled with the spirit, she was bound to go looking for her own love. I saw our mother in a way I never expected and took off running. Facing oncoming traffic, meeting the patrolling eyes of drivers behind the wheel.

Yet who couldn't love Dundee? Tiny little man. Of this world and not of this world. Potentially deaf (we weren't sure, thirteen months and he hardly made a sound) and so to my way of thinking, hearing only the music of the spheres. The spheres— where he came from, in whatever corner of heaven people are concocted, all God's created masses. Was it only I who imagined this heavenly factory? And now, let us make a new baby! And now, let us allow it to be born way too soon, and let us watch to see how it thrives, or doesn't.

Was it an accident or was it on purpose that we even had Dundee?

Was it an accident or on purpose that I was born a Cooper?

AT FIRST IT WAS kind of cute, those gurgling noises. Just listen to him, Carlotta said, isn't it sweet, Dundee knows we're going to a waterfall! She wanted so much to believe. Dundee's head wobbled from side to side, and he blew bubbles. Isn't he cute? She tried walking beside the stroller, but the trail was too narrow, so she walked ahead, slipping on muddy rocks. Which is why she didn't see the change in Dundee's face, didn't notice when he went from gurgling to wheezing, the phlegm nesting in his lungs.

The trail grew more treacherous, it was one foot in front of the other, rock to rock to rock. Even a mountain goat would've had a hard time. Hikers passed us wearing hiking boots and fleece jackets. They looked like professionals, they knew what they were doing. But not us. I watched our mother lift her baggy blue skirt to keep from tripping on it, and the sight of her pale, cold legs and her slouchy socks and black shoes embarrassed me. Just as the stroller embarrassed me. James gripped its curved handles and fought it, and as I knew it would, the stroller began to break, its cheap aluminum frame bending before my eyes.

Forest to our right, Fiery Gizzard Creek to our left. Clear, cold water at the bottom of a steep ravine. If only this water had been steamy hot, like at Yellowstone. If only Carlotta and James had said, let's go to Yellowstone, although it was a trip we would never take, not in a zillion years. (You can see the entire world from your own chair, our mother claimed, thumping her yard sale homeschool text.) Yellowstone because what Dundee really needed was steam. To open his lungs, to let him breathe. But there is no steam in Tennessee. Yellowstone, yes. Baden-Baden, yes. Greenland, Iceland, Fiji, Bali, Nepal. Hot springs all over the world, beautiful steamy waterfalls. Even in Arkansas, even in Georgia and South Dakota and Hawaii. But not Tennessee.

What those yard sale textbooks taught me.

Our father stabbed at rocks with a walking stick he'd found, and Chrissie hopped along behind him, balancing herself against our mother's big hip. Carlotta resumed humming. *Blessed Assurance: perfect submission, perfect delight.* She picked her way along the trail in her own fantasy dream, one foot in front of the other, to God be the glory. But then the stroller fell apart. From behind I saw its wheels cave inward and its umbrella seat, with Dundee inside, fold over on itself. James cursed, *damned stroller piece of shit*, and Carlotta turned in time to see Dundee's lips turn the color of a blue bruise.

I should have said something was wrong with him; I was right there, two steps behind. But the creek was opening up a little, and I could detect the sound of rushing water. Falling water. We were drawing closer—to what, I wasn't sure. A joining of hands, maybe, and devout, muttering prayer. Then some sandwiches. Then, because it's something our mother always wanted to do, but not our father, not ever our father, we might try a little hymn-sing. But only if we were blessed to be alone, because who wants to be seen standing by a waterfall singing a hymn like a crazy person?

James lifted Dundee from the stroller, and Dundee started

crying and sucking in each breath like a baby who's been crying a long, long time. Shhh, Dunny, said Carlotta. She circled her arms around James, her chubby teenage husband, the boy she'd submitted to at fourteen, like a rabbit, and hugged him and Dundee at the same time. Dunny, Dunny, she said. She wiped his eyes with the back of her hand, rubbed his snotty nose with the hem of her sweater. Dunny, she said, what made you get sick? She turned to our mother. Mama, why'd he have to go and catch a bad cold? Sickness was our mother's specialty, she was pretty much the only doctor we ever had. She took Dundee up and rocked him from side to side, her hair swaying like a horsetail. Soothing him, whispering to him, picking his nose with her pinkie.

Our father grabbed the broken stroller with one hand and sailed it into the woods. Then he set his palm on Dundee's cold head and closed his eyes as if praying. He took a deep, dramatic breath. Let's keep moving, he said, we've gone too far to turn around now.

Frank Cooper. The reason we were what we were. The reason we lived at the end of a dusty road that was ours alone. That no one bother us. The reason we didn't go to school. That our minds not be poisoned. The reason we obeyed him. That we not be spoiled.

When I was little I thought of him as Abraham. In our church in the hills he'd sit uncomfortably in the pew, the folds of his neck squeezed into his shirt collar and his sleeves riding halfway up his arms. He had a tan face and a pink neck. An outdoors man, not an indoors man, something I was proud of. At least I was proud then. But in church he always had a wary look, as if the preacher might call on him. And then one time he did.

The preacher said, Frank Cooper, are you saved? We felt a sudden shock. Who would dare call on our father? I could feel our mother tremble, sympathy mixed with shame. He cleared his throat and said, that's between me and the Lord.

We got in the truck, and he started the motor. We can have church at home, our mother said, but he didn't reply. Wherever two or more are gathered, she said.

This was before Chrissie—I had that to look forward to— but I was old enough to know what he was feeling. All those church people, he couldn't stand them, they were so happy and so blessed. They stood when it was time to stand and sat when it was time to sit, and they took out their hymnals, flipped the pages to the right song, and started singing. Even then I knew he hated them because he couldn't read the words.

You can travel the whole world in a book, our mother said, you don't even have to leave your chair! And he said, what I see with my own eyes is all the world I need, Christine. Twice a week he rode a mower over grave markers at the perpetual care cemetery, his job, and memorized names he couldn't read, which ones had crosses beside them, which ones had angels. Our mother said, and then there's the world of the spirit, Frank, what none of us can see with our eyes. And he said, no need to remind me.

He had James carry Dundee the rest of the way. The baby lay still, his cheek pressed against the cold zipper of James's jacket. Through the woods a veil of sunlight poured over us—vernal light, the equinox. Night and day the same, like magic. Little buds on trees, green shoots poking through dry leaves. Now and then Dundee coughed and whimpered. We took turns stopping to look at him. You could see his chest cave in. Chrissie thought he might need a bottle, but our mother feared he might choke.

Carlotta kept digging into her bag. She'd looped the strap across her chest to keep it from falling off her shoulder. She dug around without pulling anything out. Prayer beads, or the angel she'd carved.

A group of hikers came toward us, headed back to the trailhead. Two girls and two guys and a big dog with a leash circling its nose. We stepped aside to let them pass, and the dog promptly lunged. It was going after Dundee, trying to catch a whiff of him, but the guy holding the leash yanked the dog back. One of the girls gave out a little yelp. It all happened so fast. Chrissie started to cry, and the guy with the dog said sorry, so sorry, and the girls said sorry too, and then one of them stepped over to get a peek at Dundee, just to be friendly. I expected her to say how cute he was, but she didn't say anything. Because Dundee didn't look cute, he looked sick.

Once they were out of earshot, James said he would've killed the dog if he'd had to, and our father said he was thinking the same thing. A good reason to carry a knife, he said. You never know. Chrissie couldn't stop crying. At first it was all about what might've happened to Dundee if the dog had bit him, but then it was about the dog—what if James had killed it?—and then it was about being tired and having to pee. Our mother led her into the forest, straight up a slope and behind underbrush to hide her from sight, but the woods were so thin we could see everything.

All the things we'd seen, the suffocating closeness. Together we shared a palace: three entire rooms. Sofa and recliner in the front room, bed in the middle room, cook stove and kitchen table in the back. Outside, a privy and a cold trickling spring. We learned to creep in the dark, to feel our way with the soles of our feet. We learned how to sleep four in a bed. How to curl in a recliner like a dog. How to gather water in a plastic tub, take a drink from the tub and then wash dishes in the same tub. How to judge time by the color of the sky.

This was us—could anyone tell?

Some afternoons when no one was watching, our mother tucked away in the bedroom nursing Chrissie and our father out at his job, I'd leave Carlotta and walk up our drive just to see how far I could go, what I could get away with. After some time I built the nerve to walk as far as the state road, and I followed it for about two miles. I was maybe thirteen then. A few houses, some mobile homes in a field. Propane tanks, cars on blocks, dogs chained to trees. The curves in the road suggested an old cow path. I'd walk until I got tired, then head home prepared to say I'd been out hunting squirrels. I kept wanting to meet somebody. One day I got up the nerve to cross the road and face oncoming cars, the few that came. I feebly waved my thumb. The first man who stopped for me was a salesman driving a black van. He asked me where I was headed, and I didn't know what to say. Then I got in.

BY THE TIME WE reached the waterfall, it began to look like Dundee might not make it. His eyes had turned glassy, and his skin was hot with fever, and no matter how much James hugged him, holding him close, he wouldn't stop wheezing. We stood around him in the light-filled opening the waterfall provided. Before us, the creek spilled over a table of black rocks in pure, clear ribbons. It was the first waterfall I'd ever seen, probably the first and only one our father and mother had ever seen. But we were fools to be there. Dundee had begun fighting for air, and it felt like we were doomed. Carlotta shivered as if she were standing in snow. Pregnant, although she barely showed, and grieving already. This was not what was supposed to happen. She had made such hopeful, happy plans.

Our mother began to pray. She said, oh Lord, come heal this baby.

We weren't alone. Girls with phones stepped precariously over rocks, trying not to get their feet wet. They looked Chinese. I wondered how they got here. Like us, they weren't dressed for a hike; one of them even wore sandals. They tiptoed, then stopped, tiptoed, then stopped. Each time they stopped, they took pictures with their phones. And then there were the boys. They waded above us along the crest of the waterfall, pants wet to their knees. Somewhere along the way they'd dropped their hatchets and machetes and their stupid bush axe. When Carlotta started to cry loud enough for them to hear, they stopped and looked at us as if in awe. We made a sad tableau. Carlotta fell onto James's chest, clutched at Dundee, and sobbed.

Had she already begun thinking it was her fault? In the back of her mind, had she already begun blaming our parents, and James, and me? Because later this would come, the blame.

We formed a huddle. Our mother began speaking in tongues; it was like she was mixing French and Portuguese and Urdu, and James and Carlotta began chanting a prayer. I took Chrissie's hand and led her aside. I didn't want her to see this. Also I didn't want to meet the eyes of our father, our pillar of salt.

Carlotta, he said. Take out your phone and call 9-1-1.

She fumbled in her bag and took out her phone. She stabbed the screen, then held the phone to her ear. Stabbed again, stabbed and stabbed.

He snatched the phone out of her hand and stared at it.

There's no service here, James said.

A look of disbelief came across his face.

I saw satellites. High above, they circled the earth, hundreds of them, thousands. They had beeping little lights and antennas, searching, listening. But not listening to us.

The Chinese girls stopped taking pictures. In the presence of what might be tragedy, they looked terrified. The boys, though, seemed to think Carlotta was crying for help. They splashed back across the high table of rocks, heading, it looked like, to the path in the woods that had led them to the top in the first place. They were heading back down. To us.

I held Chrissie's hand. She wanted to know what was wrong with Dundee—was he going to die? No, I told her, he just has a very bad cold. Which was true, it was just a very bad cold, but Dundee wasn't a normal baby, his lungs were weak. An emergency, 9-1-1, if only we had the means to call. This, I didn't say. Instead I said, he'll be okay But he wouldn't be. In minutes, he would be gone.

The boys emerged from the woods to see if they could be of assistance. That's how they put it: can we be of assistance? Carlotta and James shielded Dundee from view, and Chrissie moved behind me, clinging to my leg. At home there were few strangers we ever saw. One of the boys said, is that a baby? And our father said, that's right. And we don't need none of your help, thank you.

Out of nowhere, there came the weirdest sound, a kind of chirp. Carlotta looked down at Dundee, limp and enfolded in James's arms. One of the boys said, it sounds like croup there. I used to get it when I was a kid.

Another said, could be he needs a hot shower, that's what you do for croup. Or maybe he's got a case of pneumonia.

Our father gave them a hard, cold look. This baby don't need no shower.

But the boy wouldn't stop talking. Now it was about steam. Steam, hot steam. So the baby can breathe, he said. That's what we always did. Sometimes my grandma would take me in the bathroom and turn on the faucet and....

One of the other boys interrupted him. Or you could breathe on him! Breath is the same as steam, ain't it?

The boys pushed in closer so they could see Dundee's face. I could sense Carlotta's panic. I pictured one of them putting his mouth on Dundee's mouth, the sour breath.

Our father lifted out his knife. Not one step closer, he said.

Whoa, one of the boys said, easy. He held up his hands. We were just trying to help. When the others turned to run, he ran too.

We watched them go. In about ten seconds, they were out of sight. I looked around at the waterfall and the bright, sparkling pool. The girls, too, seemed to have disappeared. Hiding in the trees, maybe, looking at us. The waterfall gushed soothingly. Unless there came a terrible drought some time, it would gush forever.

Our father walked over to James, pried open his arms, and lowered his mouth to Dundee's blue lips. Too late.

THE LAST TIME I took to the state highway, I wasn't paying attention, and I held out my thumb before I knew what was coming. So I didn't recognize the truck before it was too late. The battered, rusted front bumper and the cracked windshield. The truck slowed, and I quickly turned and kept walking. Behind my back I could hear the motor wind down, and then the sound of crunching gravel. The truck had pulled to a stop.

Came the dreaded voice: hitchhiking?

I kept walking.

Don't walk away from me. I can get you.

I turned to face my father. I felt my legs wobble.

Well, get in, he said, but not in the front. You'll go in the truck bed, where you belong. You want to act like trash, then you'll ride like trash.

I climbed in and scrambled to the front of the bed so I could crouch out of his sight while he drove.

The road whizzed by, sunlight blinding my eyes. The smell of dirty exhaust, the sound of the old chassis squeaking through the curves. The pot-holed driveway into the cemetery.

For hours, he made me sit there in the truck while he worked. If I see you try to get out, he said, I'll beat your ass.

I watched him wind his tractor over the grounds. He dodged the tombstones, rolled straight over all those flat brass plates. All the elderly and the terminally sick and the fatally injured. All the little angels and doves. When he was done, he rolled the tractor back into its shed and walked slowly to the truck. He laid his elbows over the rear gate and glared at me with his clear gray eyes. He spit into the truck bed, leaving a white glob. Then he said: You better not be looking for what I think you are, because if so, you might as well be dead.

I didn't go looking anymore. Not until after we lost Dundee.

Then I couldn't stop looking. In disbelief I walked out the door and headed toward the highway, where I'd take my chances.

FALL

A confluence of events, a torrent, a river: small tragedies, one after another, starting when Gina lost her position at the veterinarian, followed by her subsequent move home, a humiliation at thirty, and then her father's back. Now that he could hardly walk, her mother often had to help him dress, hold him steady while he went hunch-backed down the stairs, even feed him in bed sometimes. Then there was the tree. The big poplar next door was visibly dying. Three weeks after Gina moved home, an enormous limb fell into the front yard. A clear blue day in late June, and boom. The ground shook. Branches filled the yard, darkening the windows. It was as if they'd just moved into a tree house. When the man came to clear the debris, a bee zipped from the ground and stung his lip.

Gina's parents, Coy and Lynette Delacorte, had been forced to hire the tree man themselves, since the limb had fallen into their yard, not the Toomeys' yard. The Toomeys, the odd, rambling

Toomeys. With a camper in their back yard and a sorry row of faded floor mats hanging over their back fence. According to the law, the falling limb was considered an Act of God. A fine blessing for the Toomeys, whose house was now under foreclosure, but a curse for the Delacortes, who had their own share of misery.

So it went. June became July, and then August, the usual furnace. Hurricane weather. Nights, Gina sat upstairs in her old bedroom with the high school yearbooks on her closet shelf wondering what had become of her life. She could hear her parents down the hall speaking in low tones. *Prop me up on that pillow, will you? Go check the thermostat.* Sometimes, despite the heat, she opened her windows and leaned out to hear distant music. Drums, a guitar. It was the loneliest sound, yet sexy. She lay on her bed and felt her belongings (her actual belongings, not her old childhood stuff) moldering in her parents' garage. She tried to remember what was out there, tried to picture what her apartment used to contain. Gone the potted cacti, gone the kitchen décor. The rug from the Pottery Barn sour now, a cat having slipped into the garage and peed. And the cardboard boxes filled with books and pots and pans: limp, caving in. Soon enough her mother would call for help. *Your dad has to use the bathroom!* It was all so pitiful that, some evenings after supper, her dad having been fed his tray, she was tempted to just play games on her phone and drink. But she did not. Instead, unbeknownst to everyone, especially her parents, she took molly.

Molly, molly. What a pretty name. The first time someone asked her if she wanted to do molly, she didn't know what they meant. Do molly? She pictured something soft and small, like a doughnut hole. Or rather she pictured turning into something soft and small, floating and fluffy. "Molly, you know, ecstasy, the love drug." All you had to do was open the capsule, pour out the drug, draw it in a line, and snort. Or just swallow, you could do that too. Gina felt a flash of doubt—she would be jumping into oblivion—but she said of course, let's do molly. The music swelled, the crowd was thick and happy. They were at a dance party, and she was made new.

A few days ago, she was able to get some, thanks to a connection. She shouldn't have, but she did. Because who does molly alone? With no dancing, no lights, no one to share it with. But what do you do when you're home alone with your mom and dad and you're thirty years old with no hope? A life, she didn't want her parents to know, that had pretty much been ruined. So it would be MDMA, molly, the therapy drug. It was all she had left. She put in her earbuds, laid down the drug, and let the music fill her brain. Off she went.

DOWN THE HALL, IN view of the windows in Coy Delacorte's bedroom, the moon was rising. He could see it from his bed, a chipped pearl of a moon, a waxing gibbous. This was the sort of thing he took note of. In the mornings before his back injury he liked to step outside to get the paper and take time to look for the moon, faint and receding, in the empty sky. A sign of time's flow, sun and moon, one and then the other. Lines from the Daily Evening Prayer came to him—*Thine is the day, O God, thine also the night; thou has established the moon and the sun.* He could afford to feel prayerful back then, when he didn't have a slipped disk. He could look up at the white shadow of a morning moon and feel grateful. He had an open spot in his heart, room to spare in mind and body. Now all he wanted was to roll over in bed without pain, to rise out of bed and get dressed, mindlessly. To go outside and mow the grass, to sweat! Maybe even go for a run in the August heat.

He was too much of an old seminary student not to hear scripture, even now. Passages floated in his brain like smoke in a sanctuary. *My grace is sufficient for thee, for my strength is made perfect in weakness.* He was weak, yes, but then there was Gina. In June she'd arrived home disheveled and jittery, rolling in behind the wheel of her faded pickup. She opened the door and looked up at him with wet eyes. "Hey Dad." He watched her get out. Sauce-stained tee shirt, dirty feet in flip-flops, toenails painted black. He went in for a hug, to which she let out a dramatic sigh, drooping beneath a cloud of defeat. "This is it," she said, "I'm back."

Even then he knew this would be a scene he wouldn't be able to forget, one of those moments that stick with you forever, like the day when he was a teenager and he came home from a summer overseas and his mom told him she'd been diagnosed with cancer while he was gone, and he looked at her standing there, her lip trembling, her voice cracking, and he hoped she wouldn't cry. But she did, she started crying, and then she sobbed. "I might…die." Except this was Gina standing in front of him now, his baby, his only child. She didn't have cancer, but she wasn't fully well. She looked frail and diminished. Her skin had broken out with acne, and her hair was so tangled that there was a kind of nest at the back of her head. "I had to bring everything," she said, and then her voice trailed off. They walked around the truck. There was her little coffee table and armchair and lamps with no shades and a box with nothing but coat hangers and other boxes with dishes in them, and then all this unrecognizable stuff like black trash bags crammed full. It was as if a crazy person had hurled it in and driven away.

He offered to unpack the truck for her. "Go on, you need some rest," he told her. "Your mother will want to see you." What he had to do was, move stuff out of the garage and move stuff in. Rearrange everything, shift things around, start piling the boxes one on top of the other—he hadn't realized how many there were, underneath all those trash bags. He left room for the heavy things, her bed (no mattress, she must've gotten rid of it) and her armchair and all that, but he didn't get very far. The pain when he twisted his back, the sensation of bone against bone, was like a shot of flame.

He'd gone to a trail of doctors, was prescribed prednisone and Vicodin and Percocet. He stayed in bed for a full week and a half, but then he was told to get out of bed. Lying around was the worst thing he could do, they said, so he got up, slowly. One leg at a time. Walked across the bedroom like Quasimodo. Couldn't stand upright for the pain. Surgery was discussed, which seemed like a relief to him. Anything to get better. But Lynette talked him out of it. She said of course they want to do surgery! The more procedures they do, the more they profit, that's their livelihood. To which he said, just like you bring lawsuits. You're an attorney, he said, that's what you do. To which she said he was lucky he'd just recently retired, since if he hadn't he would've lost his job by now, the way he'd been laid up at home so long. She of no sympathy, rugged to the core.

A door slammed downstairs. Lynette, home from a long day at the office. Slowly, with concentration, he sat up in bed, turned, and lowered his feet to the floor. Left foot, right foot. It was the right one that was numb, like a tingly fuzzy slipper sock. He felt his temper rise. Ah, thank you, Gina. Thank you for bringing me your entire apartment crammed into a truck. And thank you, Lynette, for providing a steady income and for acting as whip-cracker in the household. And thank you, Percocet, which makes daily life manageable. He stood and took two small steps toward the window so he could spot Lynette's car in the street. But it wasn't there. Instead there was Gina, flitting in the open like a little girl, her steps gentle and liquid, like a fairy. Barefoot, under the streetlight, then gone.

WHITE RAYS OF SUN/MOON/STREETLIGHT, asphalt shadows, swaying boughs. Queens Lake, Queens Lake, Queens Lake. This the same street she learned to ride a bike on, wobbly tires, wiggling handlebars, pump, pump, pump, this the same neighborhood her school bus rumbled through, year after year, these the same neighbors who bought her Girl Scout cookies and later peeked out at her from their windows. The world was a drum. Just beyond those trees, or maybe high up in the trees themselves, wasn't that a drum/drums? The thumping bass of a drum, foot on pedal, the tin hammer of a high hat, and the cymbal—she-shing! Drums these were. Feet on pavement following the sound, the street warm to the touch. The world was a stream. A warm loving stream, water swirling around the ankles. Ankles of the world. Ankles of all the people of the world.

At the end of the street where it turned into a cul-de-sac Gina rounded the circle, her feet knowing the way by instinct, as if Queens Lake had been imbedded in her memory at the same time she learned the sound of her mother's voice. She was born, fed at the breast, swaddled, diapered and plunked into a car seat to be taken to Queens Lake. A gentle sun shone in the windows as the car turned into the drive. Here you are, little baby Gina, home.

Through the walls of a sad, shuttered house the drum beat loudly. She stood out in the street and listened, her heart keeping time. Someone was practicing inside, just one lone drummer, drumming—Tommy Ramone, Dave Grohl, John Bonham, it could be any one of them drumming in the old rancher, and she was their chosen audience. In a corner of her brain Gina knew the tune. In another corner of her brain she knew she was high. With molly, her abiding, healing friend. Trees swayed lovingly above her head. There were corridors up there. Her brain contained corridors, corners, rooms, a giant house. She ought to stay put, a voice told her in this house of her brain. But another voice, an expansive, world-welcoming voice, told her she was being invited in. Come, hear the drumming. So she walked up to the door, looked for a doorbell, and not seeing one, knocked. Timidly at first, then louder. The drum carried on. Knock, knock. She knocked until her knuckles turned sore. Knock-knock-knock, and then it occurred to her: these were the Toomeys, the hippie mom and dad and their little boy she used to babysit. Of course, David Toomey, next door! Ina-gadda-david-a.

The drum stopped. Footsteps, an opening door. An abrupt light, a face. A bearded, Jesus face. "I'm sorry?" he said tentatively, and she said, "Oh," and he said, "Can I help you?" and she said, "Maybe." As if they were dancing. She began to laugh, her mouth making a burbling, chuckling sound she'd never heard before. She said, "It's as if we're dancing!"

"Do I know you?" he asked, and she answered, "In a way, kind of you do."

The world was becoming marvelously absurd. She used to wash his sippy cup.

When the door closed, it felt like a long blink. The sensation of a yellow welcoming light, then darkness. Goodbye. Standing at the closed door she waited for the sound of the drum again, but it never came. Tree frogs rang in the hollow air. Maybe there hadn't been a drum at all. Out in the street, beneath the mothy streetlight, she turned toward home, warm bare feet on the pavement. Footstep, footstep. Maybe there hadn't even been a David.

HER JOB, COY AND Lynette had decided, would be as caregiver. Coy was recuperating more slowly than they'd hoped, and they worried that if he were alone and had a setback, no one would be there to help him. They considered one of those emergency lanyards shut-ins wear around their neck, but Coy refused. All he needed was Gina to stay close by. In case.

Deep down, he considered this a blessing in disguise. Now he could show Gina how much he cared for her; he could get to know her as an equal, as an adult. She'd been distant for so long, five hours upstate, rarely in touch. He imagined taking slow walks with her in the neighborhood. She could tell him about her life. They could share ideas, maybe read the same books and talk about them. He could lead her to books, in fact. She'd never really read them before.

Sometimes when he thought back on Gina when she was a little girl, he'd feel deep pain. Life was tough for her then, as she was always a step off. It hurt to put it this way, even in his private thoughts. (We are, he believed, what we think.) But

Gina was a step off—had been since she was little. In the years while Lynette was studying law, he was the one who went to the teacher conferences, the band concerts, the end-of-the-year awards ceremonies where nearly every kid except Gina walked onto the pathetic little stage in the gym to receive a certificate. His blood would boil—couldn't they give her anything? And then he'd experience something like deep heartbreak as he watched Gina stand awkwardly on the top level of the portable riser, the tallest kid in the class, hovering over her peers, the boys having yet to experience a growth spurt. On the top level of the riser muttering the Pledge of Allegiance while looking up at the ceiling as if following a passing bird. At home, talking to her stuffed animals. Later, watching boy bands on television, singing along. Even later, anime cartoons and cigarettes, punk, black eyeliner, steel-toed boots. Finally a little trio of friends, for whom he wished he could feel grateful. Kirby, Danielle, Brianna. Headed straight to nowhere, said Lynette.

Somehow, because almost everybody in the world eventually finds a place to be useful, to gain some minor position in life, Gina found a job. As a veterinary assistant. It seemed like a natural fit, since she'd always loved animals. Thanks to Lynette's allergies, she'd never been able to keep anything but birds and fish, plus the iguana, but now with this job she could care for dogs and cats all day. But then she was "let go." The night she called with the news, Coy stayed up late reading books of meditation and theology, searching for answers. Were some simply born to fail? Were some destined to be alone, never touching and never touched? No man is an island unto himself—this he liked to believe.

The first couple weeks she was home had been a blur, he was so medicated, but then, as he began to feel better, he tried having a conversation. What music was she always listening to? What was her favorite kind of dog? Whatever happened to Danielle, Brianna, and Kirby? In the morning, they watched news shows together, but never more than a few minutes. She said the news got on her nerves. So what do you like, he asked, what gets you going, what inspires you? He wasn't prepared for her answer. Peace and quiet, is what she said. That's all, just peace and quiet.

THE MORNING AFTER SHE took molly, she knew to expect a crash. A night of joy, then a crash. She'd slept fitfully, dying of thirst, chewing the inside of her mouth. Then when she could no longer lie in bed, she opened her eyes to the sun. Blue holograms throbbed in her brain, and a line of music came to her: *when darkness falls.* Killswitch Engage. A bird chirped outside her window, a little buzz saw. *When darkness falls, I walk in with my own resolve.*

She could hear her parents arguing downstairs. They could argue about anything. Today it was the tree. Coy wanted to be a good neighbor and cut it down for the Toomeys. Lynette wanted to sue them for negligence. You don't want to enable people like them, she said, they need to learn to stand on their own two feet. This would be the running conversation of the summer, apparently. Lately Lynette had quit parking the car in the driveway, for fear the tree would fall on it. She'd roll up after work and park on the street about a million miles from the house. Gina wondered how the two ever married. When she was young and living at home with them, she used to try and figure it out. Her father had almost become a preacher, still wished to be, it was obvious. He was always reading about God. Her mother had achieved the miracle of becoming a practicing attorney after years of homemaking and taking night courses, and she would never let you forget it, the price she paid.

Everybody paid a price at some point in their lives, though; Gina knew this better than anybody.

The night she'd agreed to go to the vet clinic after hours, she'd been so glad to be alone with a guy that she stopped on the way to pick up champagne. She would spend the evening with Rodney, the kennel attendant, the only person who was authorized to be at the vet clinic on a Saturday night. She considered what would happen if she got caught, if for some reason one of the doctors stopped in and found her there. But this wouldn't happen—the docs never visited the clinic on a Saturday night. She and Rodney would have the run of the place.

He met her at the door with a look on his face that said we can do anything we want. She handed him the champagne, and together they went back to the refrigerator to chill it. Rodney nestled the champagne between a jar of mixed carporfen and a locked box of hydrated Telazol. Animal drugs. Carporfen for pain, Telazol for putting them down. He handed her a cold beer he'd brought. I always come prepared, he said. He turned on the clinic's music, changed the station to Beck. They wandered around the premises drinking their beers, then went back to the boarding kennel to speak to all the dogs. It was a full house. The dogs rose to life, barking, shoving their noses through the rungs of their cages as Gina and Rodney walked through. Rodney was partial to a liver-colored pit bull named Oz. If I could have any dog, he'd be the one, he said. I'd take him if I could.

They got more beer and wandered back into the clinic as if they'd never been there before, looking at stuff. Rodney was drawn to muzzles, control poles, heavy gloves, squeeze cages—all the tools of restraint. Gina was slow to interpret him. He pulled on the heavy gloves, tucked a nylon leash in one pocket, moved in to pretend he was about to muzzle her. Before, she'd judged Rodney to be a little crazy but harmless. Now she wasn't so sure. She kept to the other side of the room while he opened drawers randomly. She started out to the lobby. But as she turned to go, he followed her so closely that she could hear him breathe. Next to the reception desk he wrapped both arms around her and dug his fingers into her waist. Gotcha.

The thing was, she had become desperate by then. She just needed someone to pay attention to her, someone to talk to her, maybe even love her. Don't, she said, prying his fingers loose, but then she added: not that way.

They went back to the refrigerator and popped open the champagne. Rodney handed the bottle to her, and she drank. Bubbles fizzed in her nostrils. She handed him the bottle, and he took a long swallow. He said he was twenty-one. Gina lied, said she was twenty-six. Even that seemed old to him. He'd dropped out of community college; she'd barely graduated. Not loving school—they had that in common anyway. Then he asked her, what do you do for fun, what's your "gig"? She didn't have a gig, she said, the vet hospital was her gig, animals were her gig, music was her gig. Sci-fi was kind of her gig, and movies.

He watched her closely. Anything else?

Before she could answer, he pressed a hand behind her neck and pulled her to him, kissing her deeply. He had sweet, smoky breath and soft stubble. She wondered what he'd been doing before she got here. He held her close, almost dancing with her, and as he rocked her from side to side he began easing his hands down her thighs. As if she were suddenly given the power to see what they were doing from afar, to see from above like the security camera she just remembered, the silvery black eye in the corner of the lobby ceiling she assumed had been switched off, she felt a flash of alarm. They could be caught. But wasn't this what she'd hoped for? Not getting caught, but having sex? Hadn't she agreed to meet Rodney at the clinic, expecting it?

Not stopping, they shuffled through the clinic and out to the lobby, Rodney managing to continue kissing while also slipping two fingers down the front of her camisole, easing the straps over her shoulders and lowering it to her waist. In the middle of the room a sliver of light shone from behind the wall of charts and diplomas. Together they lay down on one of the soft benches, its cushions ripe with the odor of bleach and dander. Rodney began to burrow in, still dressed, then after some fumbling he removed his jeans, and Gina's too. Gina looked up at him with wide eyes as he revealed the leash, ready to bind her. She held out her wrists.

This was not her only shame. It was also what they did after.

Woozy, spent, they dressed and made their way back into the clinic, its light blinding them briefly, and drank what was left of the champagne. Then they entered the boarding kennel and chose two dogs: Rodney the pit bull and Gina a mixed terrier she knew. They opened the back door and walked the dogs outside. It was raining, a cold spring drizzle that had the effect of waking them up, their faces now damp and bright feeling. The dogs seemed to feel it too, free of their constraining cages. Rodney and Gina walked them across the lawn behind the vet clinic, slipped through a hedgerow, and took to the sidewalk. There were few cars. Neither of them knew the time—it could be midnight, it could be much later. The pit bull tugged hard. He was massive, barrel-chested. A born fighter, Rodney said. The two reached the intersection ahead of Gina. She could see them silhouetted against the lights, the pit bull and Rodney, leash looped short in his hand. The traffic light turned green, and in a moment of confusion Rodney stepped out into the street, stumbled, and let go of the leash. The dog bolted. Bright headlights, cars crossing, and then the dog, caught in the middle. Within seconds a delivery truck hit him, rolling him beneath its tires. The truck careened right and jumped the curb, its lights tracing a jagged arc high above the street.

By the time Gina caught up with Rodney, it was plain there was nothing either of them could do; the pit bull had died instantly, his spine broken and a deep laceration splitting his gut. The driver of the truck sat behind the wheel, his face faintly visible in the streetlight he'd come close to hitting. He lowered his chin as if looking for something in his lap. Rodney gripped Gina's arm. "Go," he said. She doubled her hold on the shivering terrier's leash, feet planted on the asphalt. "Go," he repeated, "I'll take care of it." She should walk back, shut the terrier in its cage, and…go home. He insisted on it. He had less to lose than she did; he would take the fall.

But he'd forgotten about the security camera. That night, stunned by the horror of the dog's death and the fear of what was to come, they'd both forgotten the ever-watching eye in the clinic lobby. Had it been turned off? No, it hadn't. Three months later, and Gina still lived in the shame of blurry images. As far as she knew, she'd live in the shame of those images for the rest of her life. She woke in the middle of the night and saw them. Woke again in the morning, opened her eyes, and saw them.

Went downstairs into the kitchen and saw them, the blurry film of Rodney Brite and Gina Delacorte, rated X. Her parents drank their coffee and watched the news. She glanced at the TV screen. She herself had been on the news, did they know?

"Good morning, Gina, sit down and join us. We've just been discussing the Toomeys' tree."

Gina bit her tongue, actually bit it. Her whole mouth was sore.

"That tree's completely dead now, it's going to fall," Lynette continued. "And you know when a tree falls, there's no warning. It takes no more than a second, and it's down, period, end of story. We don't even like you going out for the mail anymore."

The mail. Gina considered that the only good thing about taking care of her father was that she was the one, not him, to go to the mailbox each day. To retrieve what he didn't need to see. A care package from Rodney. Legal papers.

DAYS WENT BY, THE tree the only topic. Like a group of strangers who don't know what to say to one another, the Delacortes looked for common ground, a subject of interest they could all agree on, something to share. The tree, then. Even Gina found herself drawn in. Despite her own despair, despite her fear of being sued, herself, which might expose her shame, she began to engage in the tree debate. To sue or not to sue. To cut or not to cut. To ignore the tree, at one's great peril, or to be wary of the tree and be safe. Lynette said, you can never truly be safe! This was her default position. The tree loomed over their driveway. Deep within its trunk, slippery larvae chewed the wood to dust.

Gina said, "If it was an Act of God for the limb to fall in June, why would it not be an Act of God for the whole tree to just die, and then fall? Why can you sue the Toomeys for their dying tree but not their fallen limb?"

"We shouldn't have let them get away with that dead limb," Lynette said. "We were just being nice. The Toomeys are being negligent by not cutting down that tree. You just don't sit around and wait till it falls, for Christ sake. Let's say it falls on our car, or it falls on our house—or on *you*, Gina. Then how would the Toomeys feel? Talk about an avoidable tragedy!"

"So was it an Act of God or not, when that limb fell?"

"It was a windy night…" Coy began.

"And God makes the wind…" Gina said.

"And God made the tree!" Lynette said. "You could do that all day. God made the world! But we don't leave everything up to God. If we did, there'd be no need for law. Some things *we* control."

"So do you really plan to sue the Toomeys, the nice Toomeys? Aren't they bankrupt?"

"I don't think we really plan to sue them," Coy said.

He was interrupted by Lynette. "I do," she said. "I'm going to issue them a summons. If they don't take down that tree, then I'll force them to do it."

Gina could picture it, the summons. According to Rodney, who sent her text messages every day, it was just a matter of time. The vet clinic was losing business, for one thing. Then there was the truck driver, the one who'd hit Oz. He'd climbed out, looked down at the dog, and complained of neck pain. Gina and Rodney would be called in to testify. It would all come out, everything they did that night.

The clinic would shut down, and the tape would be public record.

When the incident happened, it made the local news. PRIZE DOG ESCAPES FROM VET CLINIC OVERNIGHT, IS RUN OVER.

Rodney claimed he'd left the back door open, said he'd propped it open when he misplaced the key. The pit bull was out, he confessed; he shouldn't have let the dog out of its cage, but he wanted to play with him. For a week, this was the story, and it seemed to be believed. Rodney was summarily fired, the dog's owners were compensated, and Gina stayed at work. But then one morning, one of the vets took down the security camera and replayed the tape. Gina + Rodney. Confronted with the truth, Gina walked out of the clinic and threw up.

I'm going to issue them a summons. How was it that life worked this way, that one person's tragedy could intersect with another's, unbeknownst to both, like that guy getting stabbed at the Rolling Stones concert while another guy drowned there that same night, both of them just wanting to hear music? Or like two people at a doctor's office in the waiting room, side by side, about to hear the same devastating news?

Gina went to the kitchen window and looked out at the Toomeys' house. It appeared dark, even in the bright light of day, its window screens blackened with age. It occurred to her that the windows were wide open in the heat. They weren't running their air conditioning. Maybe they didn't turn on any lights. Something bad had clearly happened to them along the way. They couldn't even pay their mortgage. Funny how everybody seemed to know. So their life sucked too.

At least they still had a house. Not only did she not have a house, or an apartment anymore, she didn't have a job anymore either. Probably wouldn't be able to get another job, ever. With her record, not even a dirty little convenience store would hire her. She looked into her future and saw nothing. A black tunnel of nothing. The Toomeys, though: at least they had their music. There they were, sitting in their hot, dark, foreclosed-upon house, hitting the drums and playing the bass in a hippie version of the Von Trapps. She was sure it was Mr. Toomey on the bass. He used to teach lessons back in the day.

All she had was her parents, to whom she was an alien, and Rodney, who wouldn't stop sending her messages. They were in this together, he said. It was his fault; he shouldn't have made her do the things he did.

Don't talk about it anymore, she texted back. And never ever call.

What can I do, I want to make it up to you.

Send me molly.

THE SUMMONS CAME A week later by way of a sheriff's deputy. Coy was the one to answer the door: mud-grey uniform, bright badge. "I'm here to serve a summons for Gina Delacorte." As if by clairvoyance she'd known he was coming, Gina appeared in the doorway. The deputy asked for identification, and she had it ready. Then without saying a word she took the summons from the deputy's hand and vanished.

It happened so fast that Coy wasn't sure if he'd imagined it. Afterwards he stood and watched the deputy's car pull away, its whipping antenna. He felt a nerve tingle in the back of his neck. Something big had just happened, but he wasn't sure what. In his mind, there was now a permanent snapshot of Gina's fingers pinching a yellow, yellow envelope. Already she was back in her room, sequestered again in the inner sanctum she had created for herself when she first arrived in June. Back then he'd been glad for it, the room she could retreat to, glad for the chance to care for her again, like a child. But she'd become a mystery, and as the summer went by he'd grown afraid to talk to her.

He crept up the stairs. He considered knocking on her door but thought better of it. Not knowing what to do with himself, he went to his room to lie down, to hear her if she cried or called out. Her trouble, whatever it was, had left him shattered, and he fought the urge to rush into her room and swallow her in an unaccustomed embrace. Now more than ever he was sure he'd do anything for her, anything. It was cloudy outside, the late-day light low and gray. He was glad Lynette was at work, and he prayed she'd be tied up at her desk for a long time. He listened for any sign of Gina, tried to imagine what she was doing in her room. He pictured her sitting on her bed reading the summons. Or she'd read it, and now she was lying down, her face buried in her pillow.

How utterly impossible it was that she, of all people, would be in trouble. Nothing in her whole life's experience suggested she'd ever be. She was the timid one at every party, hanging against the wall—had never even had a date as far as he knew. There were times he'd actually wished she'd get in trouble! But now that she was, he wished the opposite for her. That she could be happy, that life could be good to her, and fun, and easy.

A blast of music startled him to his feet. After such pro-longed silence, the sound consumed the house, the high wail of a stratocaster, drums and bass. It was all so sudden and so loud that he immediately feared she was on the verge of destroying something—her room, herself. Something is about to break, he thought, things are going to fly. But then he heard Gina's voice. Not crying, not shouting, but singing. He went to her door and opened it. Through the tears in her eyes, she smiled at him. "Dad." She took the summons from her bed and handed it to him. "See," she said, "it's not about the tree."

In his heart he had told himself he'd do anything for her, and he would, he told himself again, he would, he would. He held the summons in his hands, and the words blurred before his eyes. She would have to appear in court. "Just come with me," she said. "Let's go around the neighborhood on a walk, like old times." She kept crying and smiling at once, like a happy crazy person. She slipped a little pill in his hand. White, maybe an aspirin. "For your back, to help you walk."

He'd do anything, so he swallowed it.

On the news, they'd said they were in for a storm. They were tracking it off the coast, a Category 1 they'd named Fay. The name made Gina laugh. We're going out to meet Fay, she said. Come on, dad. The trees of the neighborhood swayed wildly, their thick summer foliage fanning the sky. Queens Lake, Queens Lake. She took his arm, and he faltered. Soon you'll feel fine, she said. Come, I'll go slow with you. She made her steps tiny. See? A little bit at a time.

Coy felt himself turning strange. The wind grew louder in his ears. Out in the street, a garbage can tumbled by. He shouted Gina's name. In his mind he added a question—what did you do?—but he wasn't sure whether the question made it out of his mouth. There she was, keeping him steady. What did you do, what did you do, love.

In her hours alone Gina had fallen so low that she knew she could survive only by being high, by succumbing to the psychotropic healing of ecstacy, MDMA, molly. It made her happy, and she'd wanted so much to be happy with somebody.

Love—did her father say love?

They'd arrived at the tree. They hadn't had to travel far to get here. Oh holy tree, she whispered, blessed holy tree! Heavy, fat raindrops began to fall. She lifted her face. Come, let's go under.

He paid no attention to the tree, or the rain. Instead he focused on Gina. No matter what she did.

She dropped to her knees, then fell flat on her back. Dad, say something to the tree!

The pain of getting to his knees, then to lie prone on the hard ground, inch by inch, spine curling like a monkey's. He heard the tree lean into the oncoming gusts, its old limbs cracking. His ears were like radar, he could hear anything in the world. And his arms—how prickly this summer grass, how prickly and tickly.

I, BILLIE, SEND YOU ON

Let me dip my fingers into your familiar head of hair, Nita. Let me feel for the final time the shape of your skull, the way it curves over a flat ridge and smooths down to the neck. Let me fix your hair even here, Nita, in this sad excuse for a beauty parlor with its buzzing overhead light. And down the hall, the men whispering to each other, dressed like crows.

To such do we finally go.

How quickly the smell of your cigarette smoke fades from the world! How quickly all that smoke from your Kent Lights embedded in your sweaters, your skin, your hair fades away. All those twenty-one years of Fridays in my chair, the smoke announcing you'd arrived. Now we have the scent of green apples flowing through the heating vents.

The smoke in your voice also gone. The hoarse cough in your words when you told me you'd had enough of your old life, you'd "had it" with Terrence. But where could you go, you said. You threw up your hands. I know, I said, where could you? And where, for that matter, could I? So I said, lay your head back and tell me if the water's too hot.

The secrets we shared and nobody knew. Nor shall they ever, sweet, although when Terrence brought over your clothes—for eternity!—and he neglected panties and shoes, I wanted to take his arm and squeeze him hard, dig in my nails and ask him what did he think, burying his wife barefooted.

All those stories we shared about him over the years. Terrence—he was good enough, it's true. A good provider, a good sport. He never betrayed you. But when you're not a true match, you're not a true match. This is the cold truth we came to know. Your Terrence, my bland Allen. Remember how we laughed about them in the middle of the salon? Tears rolled down your face. Remember the time I put you under the dryer to let you really cry? The hood shielded you from shame.

Now let me lay your head back one last time. No need for water now—this sink's dry. I just need a way to prop you up. Let me do your hair one last time, bangs curled and brushed back the way you like them, concealing the coming gray. Later, when I tuck you into the pleated white suit he brought, I'll slide your feet into a pair of my flats. Just as, once, I slid beside you in our hotel dream.

THE AFTER-LIFE

n those days we gathered in the parlor for the mail. The post-
man stuffed mailboxes without speaking to us, and our hearts
either rose or fell. Later the payphone in the hallway would
ring, and one of the girls would answer. You could hear her
from your bed. *Hello? Oh hey.* Sometimes the phone would ring
and ring, and I'd go answer. It was him again. His crusty voice
betrayed his age.

How's my girl today?

Men circled the college in their cars, alone, slowly driving.
We were like candy, we were like drugs, we were the pink of
their dreams. Five hundred single girls sleeping in little rooms,
windows open to the fresh air.

My girl, my man said, tell me what you've been up to.

I never meant to talk to him so much or even learn his name.
But in those days we didn't know what we didn't know. On
weeknights after the sun went down, we withdrew into our

rooms. The hall phone rang, someone answered. Another call came, and another, always someone answering. It was our only phone. I waited my turn. As the night went on and the air fell silent and finally I heard the lone searching call, I picked up.

Tell me what you've been up to, he'd go, and I'd say something like doing my nails. So tell me what that looks like, and I'd describe my bed. Because he liked to hear about my bed. I do everything on my bed, I told him, I read and do homework and drink hot chocolate and make sandwiches and sketch in my sketchbook on my bed. Now I'm doing my nails on my bed, so I've got these little scissors and a new bottle of polish called Hot Kimono, and if I'm not careful it'll tip and ruin my bedspread. My bedspread? White with little roses, just like you imagine.

Ruby, he'd say. My made-up name. I need to meet you.

That you cannot do, I'd say, and I'd hear his cheek rub against the receiver. But you can call me tomorrow.

In those days some girls cried about not having a boyfriend, while some dropped out of college when they got one. Then there were the girls who were in love with each other. They lived in Horton Hall. I didn't know any of them, but when I passed beneath their windows it gave me something to think about.

My man said, tell me about the girls, and I'd tell him about the lesbians. Just to see what he'd say. I'd describe girls holding hands in the dark. Really, he'd say, holding hands? But then I'd tell him it's nothing, it's just friendship. Sometimes girls just want to get close to each other. Oh yeah, he'd say, and his voice would drift away. I pictured him in a dingy kitchen with a buzzing refrigerator; I had him in a chair at his kitchen table with a Formica top, his spotted hands clutching a coffee mug. A widower, retired, with no one to talk to but me.

And whose hand do you hold, he'd ask. No one's, I'd tell him. And no one is fine with me.

Not everybody is a link in a chain.

In those days you could keep to yourself and no one would ask any questions, especially if you weren't pretty. If you weren't pretty, who cared what you did in your life? In high school I invented an out-of-town lover named Marshall Smith: I was in a long-distance relationship. I bought a cheap silver ring and wore it on my thumb, a gift from Marshall. Sometimes I loved him, and sometimes I didn't, and we'd break up. I'd leave his ring on my dresser thinking I might play the field, but no one ever asked for my number. I'd catch couples kissing in the hall between classes, and my mind would race. Not my heart, mind you, my mind.

Occasionally my cousin Avery would come over to my house to get the scoop about girls. What did I know about Leslie Hofmeyer? Would she put out? How about Andrea Malone? You could say Avery and I had a unique friendship. When we were kids, we'd play fort, but when we got older, we'd play around. His idea, not mine. It was an innocent thing. Once he told me he'd figured out a way to turn his body inside out. He stood in the doorway of the bathroom and unzipped his pants. He grinned. Do you want to see? I can do it, but I have to warn you, it gets bloody.

After high school, he joined the navy. I got accepted to St. Marys and became surrounded by girls. The two down the hall who were like kittens. The ones who'd go out, then come back with hickeys. The one who liked to vacuum. And then the one named Byon, I swear she was actually a boy.

What are the girls up to, my man loved to ask. I stood in the dim, empty hall and thought how to answer. What was Byon doing, what was Shayna doing, with that hickey on her throat? I told him what he wanted to hear: we're all getting ready for bed.

I slept to the sound of bubbles in an aquarium, dreaming those floating dreams that wake you right before you hit the ground. In her bed on the other side of the room, my roommate dreamed of a boy named Philip. He'd finally asked her out. Now she packed every Friday and hit the highway, and on Sundays she returned with dry leaves buried in her sweater—they'd had picnics in the woods. So I dreamed of a thicket of trees, and whoever joined me there was always gone the moment I opened my eyes. On the phone my man would say, tell me about your dreams, and I'd make things up. I dreamed I was on a horse, I dreamed I drowned, I dreamed I lost all my teeth. He'd say, let me see you, please.

At last I gave in. Early autumn, woodsmoke in the air, a football Saturday. I watched girls run up and down the hall in flip-flops, towels wrapped over their wet hair. They stood in front of bathroom mirrors waving wands of mascara. Oh, the excitement. Outside, cars lined up, bound for Duke and Carolina. I pictured football stadiums glimmering with blue, I saw cheerleaders swishing pompoms against their thighs, so happy.

I called him, not the other way around.

I'd asked for his number weeks earlier, jotting it down. 929-6370. I nestled the slip of paper in the back of my desk drawer, and whenever I needed a pen or paper, the number was there. Bruce. Bruce-Without-A-Last-Name. Because that's what we agreed upon. No last names. Just Bruce and Ruby.

By then we'd had many talks. First it was only about me, of course. What do you like, Ruby? Dogs or cats? Winter or summer? The sound of trains, or the sound of waves? Sleeping with a night light, or sleeping in the total dark?

Tell me more about your dreams.

When I got up the nerve to ask him about his dreams, I held my breath. I thought he'd say he'd been dreaming of me...oh Ruby you know I dream of you...and he'd say he dreamed of the bed I slept upon...and the color of my sheets...my hair, my eyes...my...smell. But instead he dreamed of planets. Planets and space travel and UFOs. Because UFOs are real, he said, it's just that the government doesn't want us to know. UFOs are real, extraterrestrials are real, and dreaming is just a form of time travel. When you dream of falling it's because you actually did fall, only you can't remember when, or where, or in which dimension. Every particle in our bodies is replicated in space.

I fell in love with the way he talked. Like when he said he had polio as a kid and spent six months in an iron lung, and while he was stuck in the iron lung he wrote an entire book in his head called *The Last Battle*. But then he had a miracle cure and forgot everything.

He said he had a sister in Arkansas who was a soil scientist—her specialty was peat—and he said Johann Sebastian Bach and Frank Zappa are just two sides of a coin. He said he always wished he had a child. A baby, a little baby. He said he loved every kind of music, so I asked him if he could stand listening to the Monkees—would he listen to "The Last Train to Clarksville" over and over again? —and he said sure, I love the Monkees, Davy Jones is a friend of mine.

I didn't believe him, but I didn't care. He had a vivid mind.

I'll send a cab for you, he said, and I confessed I'd never ridden in a cab. He laughed. He said a cab, Ruby, is the ride of kings.

In a cab you sit in the back and tell the driver where to go, and that's it—off you fly.

BEAR IN MIND THAT in those days we were free. Not free of expectations or rules—in this, we were never free. But we were free to disappear. We could walk out the door and simply vanish. And this did happen, people vanished! Like Mary Hipple, who vanished from the K-Mart one Sunday. Or like that woman in the paper who drove into the parking lot at work, all the people around, and this guy just jumped in the passenger seat, held a gun to her head, and forced her to drive away. Gone. But you could also vanish on purpose. Which is what happened when I stepped outside the dorm, eyes peeled for my taxi. I felt six feet tall, powerful and magnified. Other girls huddled on the sidewalk like giddy children, waiting for their rides to Carolina. But I was waiting for a cab. I searched in the distance for a bright yellow car with a light on its roof. But when it came, the cab wasn't yellow, it was drab black, with white letters painted on the side: METROPOLITAN. The car rolled to the curb, and all eyes fell on me. Through the window I could see a cardboard box on the back seat. I looked at the driver, an oily-haired man with a wide grin on his face. He waved at the box. Sorry, he said, you can just move that over. I knew the voice.

EVERY NOW AND THEN you feel your life change. Like they say, *time froze*. I opened the door of the cab and there was a box and there was the driver, and up in the air a silver plane drew white lines in the sky. The plane stayed suspended like a toy. I hesitated.

Inside, the cab smelled like a wet wool coat. Autumn colors bled through the smudged windshield, ugly foam poked through the cracked vinyl seat. Up front: Bruce. Until that moment he was just a voice. Now he was a smiling, actual man.

You ask, what had my life been so far? Picture a mouse at the back of a drawer.

Judy, my mother used to say, you seem so sad, why don't you call somebody? She was always hoping the phone would ring— for me. When Friday nights rolled around, she'd stand there staring at me. Why don't I get you a hair appointment?

Judy.

Climb in, Ruby, he said. I pushed the box out of the way and slipped in next to it. I could feel him watching me in the mirror. Already I'd been deceived. He'd said he'd send a cab, not drive one. I squinted my eyes at the dashboard, the photo in plastic, his I.D. If only I'd worn my glasses, I could read his full name, see his credentials. Bruce _____? Bruce the taxi driver, Bruce the old man who wasn't so old after all. I regarded his thin neck, the caved-in hollow between the tendons, his oiled dark hair. He was bound to have spent time on that hair. But it wasn't bad, really; there was something a little debonair about him, a style. His voice, so hoarse and crusty—it was part of his charm, part of the reason I'd kept answering his calls. Now there he was, his long thin arm thrown casually over the front seat like a man who's out for a nice long drive.

He said, you know it's me, don't you?

Yeah. Bruce.

So we meet at last.

He pulled away from the curb, and the girls watched me go. I imagined what they might say later. *She went away in a strange*

black cab, and we never saw her again. I would become legendary.
We hardly knew her.

I scrunched against the armrest in the back seat, my mind on high alert. I watched the campus recede, one building after another, and felt my old life slip away. But who cared? By then I'd come to believe that if you hold on to your life, you'll never go anywhere. All those girls in the dorm: weren't they going nowhere? Judy, Judy, I could hear my mother say, why don't you call somebody? Well, I had. Thanks to Bruce, I finally had. I imagined introducing him. Hello, this is my man Bruce. When he was a teenager, he ran with the bulls. In Korea he nearly lost his toes to frostbite.

OF ALL THE THINGS we'd talked about on the phone, we kept coming back to the same subjects. He liked UFOs and government spies and the electric grid. I liked psychology and reincarnation. Together we wanted to uncover the ghosts of our previous lives. Bruce said he didn't believe you could come back as a lower form of life. A person doesn't die and come back as a bat, for example. Maybe, I said, but if you love bats, that would be a reward. When we finally got around to the subject of sex, Bruce said he didn't think sex was necessary. It was possible to go about your life with no urge to procreate. This was the most free idea to me. We talked about one of our favorite movies, *The African Queen*, how Humphrey Bogart wades in the river and leeches cling to his legs, how leeches, those perfect creatures, have sex with themselves.

I sat in the back of Bruce's taxi and watched him drive, one strong hand on the wheel. He turned on the radio. I looked out the window to make sure he was headed in the right direction. We were going to a cemetery called Greenwood. I'd chosen it because of its pond; getting acquainted is always easier when there's a body of water. I tucked a dinner roll in my purse in case the pond had ducks. If that failed, we could always wander among the tombstones and read the names.

Bruce pulled into the parking lot and turned off the motor. Here we are. We got out of the car and looked each other over. In the beginning I'd pictured a balding, silver head and a pudgy round body, but as time went by I didn't know what to imagine. Now there he was, the whole of him: medium tall, gaunt and sinewy, like a guy who fixes cars. I could see him disappearing beneath a truck. But he was handsome in a way, if you don't mind a strong Adam's apple. He was probably forty. White t-shirt, gray windbreaker, work pants. And a narrow belt cinched around his skinny waist. He reminded me of my uncle John Rice, who was slowly killing himself at the textile mill.

While I looked at Bruce, he stood there looking at me too. Just eyeing me. If a beam of sunlight suddenly landed on my face, I wouldn't have been surprised. I wondered what he thought of me: no makeup, navy slacks, cable knit sweater. And a beret—I couldn't help wearing my little wool beret. I felt its weight on the top of my head. In any minute, it could spontaneously combust.

We took the path from the parking lot to the pond, a shimmering hole at the bottom of a slope scattered with tombstones. White ducks, a pair of swans. I pulled the roll from my purse, and Bruce took half and I took half. Ducks swam toward us in a flotilla. Then the swans glided in, dipping their long necks. If I were a bird, I said, I'd be a swan, and Bruce said: you already are.

He proved to be clever like that; he knew what to say. *You already are*, he said, and I became a swan, transmogrified. I was filled with gratitude. It was as if he knew what I once was, a pale redheaded girl in junior high who curled her hair every night on sponge rollers. My hair flipped along the edge of my collar like a jellyroll, a perfect target for abuse. Once in history class I felt two girls approach me from behind. I sat in my desk, still as stone. There came the light touch of fingers in my hair: they were planting something. Tiny plastic rifles lifted from a diorama. Rifles. I had rifles in my hair.

We walked the edge of the pond, and the ducks paddled alongside. Every now and then, the swans would rise up in the water and chase the ducks away, and the ducks would flap their wings and quack, something we both found funny. It was easy to be with Bruce. I fought the urge to take his hand—to hold hands with him, a man! His were bony and hairless, but also delicate, like an artist's. We wandered among the oldest tombstones, and I watched him run his fingers over the faint, disappearing names of the dead. Some of the tombstones had bible verses on them. *Oh death, where is thy victory, where is thy sting?* Bruce said, if you could choose the words for your tombstone, what would they be? My mind went blank. I wanted so much to be clever like him.

He said, let me help you. Here lies….

Judy McCrae, I said without thinking.

Judy?

I mean, Ruby.

But you're really Judy?

Maybe, I said. But not with you. With you, I'm Ruby.

So here lies Judy, he said. Because she is no more.

AFTER WE'D WALKED THE cemetery, and after we'd driven out to the airport to watch planes fly in (together on the front seat of the cab), Bruce told me to get in the back seat. He said, you're in a cab, remember? I felt an unfamiliar thrill. For a second I hoped he'd climb in the back with me, but instead he shut my door and got behind the wheel. It was getting dark, time to return to the dorm. Only later did I see that he'd figured everything out ahead of time. Who was he, but a cab driver, and who was I, but his fare?

BEFORE BRUCE, I USED to linger in the dorm parlor to watch girls sign in and out. To avoid looking like a snoop I'd lay a textbook over my lap and pretend to take notes: *9:18—Janet Clarey out, with guy in plaid jacket, buckle loafers, tan socks. 9:39—Debbie and Reba out, carrying matching pocketbooks.* I'd slouch below the stairwell and feel how pathetic I must look. Sitting in a wing chair, the thin glow of a table lamp lighting my face, I was an old auntie.

We had so many rules then. Weeknight curfew: 10 p.m. Weekends: 1 a.m. Leave the dorm after 6 p.m., sign the book. Upon return, sign back in. Fail to sign out, lose the privilege of going out again for two days. Come in after curfew, lose privileges for every minute you're late. Mrs. LeHay, the dorm mother, was in charge of the book. She sat at her desk and watched everyone with her judging little eyes. When she saw that I liked to sit in the parlor alone, she deemed me her assistant. Judy, she said, I can always count on you.

But she couldn't count on me, she never could. One day I was sitting in the chair alone, and the next day I was signing the book. 7:30 p.m.—JUDY MCCRAE, OUT.

Bruce drove me to the country to look at the stars, and then he drove me there again in a driving rain, nothing but pinewoods and tobacco fields. We drove to a drugstore to look at magazines, and we drove to a flea market and bought old bottles and postcards. On a Sunday we drove all the way to the Carolina planetarium, talking about various things, every subject but the deeply personal, another one of our rules. No confessions, no digging into the past. So it was all right to tell him about my brother, how he'd been a bed wetter when he was little, how my parents pinned a sensor to his sheets so a bell would ring when he peed. Lights on, everybody up, Ted's wet the bed again! But it wasn't all right to tell him that I'd been a bed-wetter too. And it wasn't all right to tell him I was a klepto or that of all the girls in my dorm, only Byon ever talked to me. Because no one would talk to her.

Bruce loved the planetarium, but he'd forgotten they had hours. We walked round and round the building, just looking at the dome. It hadn't occurred to him they might be closed. If he could do anything (other than drive the cab, which he only did when he felt like it, and mostly he didn't), he'd be an astronomer. Imagine the astronauts who come to this planetarium, he said, this is where they learn to navigate by the stars! They lie back in chairs, and the whole cosmos is projected over their heads on a giant screen. When they go up in space and something goes wrong, they're okay because they know where they're at. They're guided by the stars.

Guided by the stars, we held hands for two hours on the highway. Fingers locked. He said he'd never seen a girl with hands as small as mine. You're a pixie, he said. Little hands, little feet. You must have been Thumbelina in your previous life.

As long as I had Bruce, I didn't need anyone else. I'd never really needed anyone before, anyway, but now I felt complete, perfected. My mother kept sending me letters. I'd enter the dorm after class and spy a white envelope propped inside my mailbox. She enclosed dollar bills for Cokes and sticks of gum. Once, I opened an envelope and found heads cut from movie star magazines, like paper coins. Look at all these hairstyles, she wrote. You would look good with any of them, but how about Claudia Cardinale?

FINALLY I AGREED TO go to Bruce's apartment. He pulled to the curb, I slid in back, and off we flew. He kept smiling at me as if a surprise was coming, looking mod in his new leather driver's cap. He'd bought it at the flea market, said it made him feel like Bob Dylan. As usual I wore my beret. In my purse I'd stuffed a clean pair of panties, just in case. In case of what, I didn't know. It was just something I'd done without allowing myself to think too much about it, sort of the way you watch your fingers steal a pack of gum at the store and you're not even sure they're your own fingers. I looked down at the empty seat. Whatever happened to that box, I asked—there used to be a box in the back, remember?—and he said he'd mailed it to a science lab. It contained a suspicious object of an alien material. There's something you ought to know, Ruby, he said: up in space there are hundreds, *thousands*, of objects orbiting the earth, and when their orbit is disrupted, they enter our atmosphere in a blaze of fire. Sometimes they flame out, and people find them. Like me. I find them. A lot.

We arrived at his apartment, the lower half of an old house

in an old neighborhood. He parked in the yard beneath a tall magnolia, and we stepped out onto a carpet of brown leaves. I looked at the house and imagined him inside, alone. This is where he was whenever we talked on the phone. After I left for Thanksgiving break, this is where he'd be. Already I knew I'd want to call him. It would have to be after midnight, when my parents and my brother were asleep. I'd go downstairs in the kitchen in the dark, where the phone was, and call.

We walked through the entryway that led to his door. He unlocked the deadbolt and stopped to look at me. Do you ever feel like you're in a dream, he asked, and nothing seems real? I nodded, or at least that's what I remember. It's been awhile. He placed one hand on my back. I felt the tips of his fingers. Well, this is one of those times—maybe this is actually a dream. Or maybe it's the after-life.

He pushed open the door, and a cat rubbed across my leg. The room was pitch-dark. He kicked the cat out of the way, calling its name. Go on, Dick Ripley. He turned on a light: in the room there were shelves jammed with books, magazines, record albums, and cloudy glass jars. I went to take down a jar. Whoa, he said, careful. Some things you just can't touch. He led me through a hallway into the kitchen, where he pulled the string on a bare light bulb. There was the kitchen table I'd imagined, and there the refrigerator. How strange, I said, I used to picture you in a kitchen just like this.

He said, maybe you've been here before and you didn't know it. Like maybe this really is just a dream. It's possible. Our minds have this way of pre-seeing. I just happen to believe it's not strange at all that you saw my kitchen in your head. Once you opened your life to me and we started talking, your mind projected outward into time/space and entered my wavelength. Each of us moves in an invisible array of energy, like a blanket. Right now, Ruby, you're wearing a blanket of energy, and because I'm tuned into you, I can feel your blanket, and I can even enter your blanket if you let me. Which you will, right? You're doing it right now, you're letting me in.

That's what he said: you're letting me in, and I was, I know I was. He was the most interesting person I had ever known. Compared to him, the whole world was dull. From Bruce I'd learned to ask questions, to be skeptical of everything. Nothing is the way it seems on the surface, he taught me; even the smallest child, barely able to talk, is a mere step away from understanding the secrets of the universe. I watched him move smoothly through the kitchen like a dancer. He opened the refrigerator, and the faint creases in his face became illuminated. I still didn't know his exact age, but by then it didn't matter to me. Ruby, he'd told me once, you are wise beyond your years, and I replied, not knowing where the words came from, *we were born alike.*

He poured his cat a bowl of milk, and we watched him as if we'd never seen a cat drink before. The kitchen was quiet except for the sound of the cat's licking tongue. Bruce whispered, I'm so glad you're finally here, there are so many things I want to show you. He left to put on a record, and I felt a queasy exhilaration. From the living room, a quiet song began. I went out and sat on the couch. An organ, with drums. Slow, sultry music that makes you want to shut your eyes. Bruce handed me the album cover. It was Shirley Scott, *Drag'em Out.* The queen of organ, nobody plays like Shirley. He drank from the bottle of malt liquor he'd taken from the refrigerator. A cabbie's cabernet, he liked to call it. He drank it all the time. I sat back and scanned the cluttered shelves, the books and albums and jars. I had to know about the jars, but he stopped me. Top secret, he said, it's a speculative project, could be enormously profitable. He put one hand on my knee. Enormously profitable, he said again. Through the front window, behind a thin purple curtain, the last light of day shone through, and the room began to feel like a forbidden, secret den.

NOW THAT I HAVE you alone with me. This, Bruce never said. *Now that you're here.* If by chance in some other dimension you'd peered into the window, through the sliver of room visible along the edge of the curtain, you would have wondered about us. About him, rather. How he'd managed to get this young girl into his apartment, and what he planned to do with her. But we were a real eye-to-eye couple. So when we rose from the couch, after an hour of talk, after two malt liquors for him and one for me (the bitter foam still on my lips), it was an agreed-upon thing. We shuffled down the hall past the kitchen. I slipped my arm around his waist and squeezed thin flesh. Shirley Scott was back at her keyboard, playing her organ for us, the volume turned up high so we could hear her from the back, in Bruce's bedroom, where I'd suggested we go.

I could feel his nervousness, or perhaps it was his eagerness, the sensation of energy barely suppressed, the urgent feel of heart-in-throat. In his room, we fell onto his unmade bed, a single mattress on a frame, and I let myself flop beneath him like a doll. In the black dark, I felt him without seeing him, bone and muscle, neck, face, breath. Then he startled me by reaching to turn on a bedside lamp. I want to see you, he said, but what he really meant was: I want to see us. Beside the bed there was a mirror screwed to the wall, room-sized, as if it had been stolen from a department store dressing room. We sat up and looked at ourselves, shiny and surprised. I watched Bruce bury his face in my hair. He lifted his eyes to the mirror and looked at me. You know I love your red hair, he said, I'd like to take a snip of it to remember you by.

Before I could answer, he pushed me down on the mattress, and we began to wrestle. Had I ever wrestled in my life? Had he? I began to suspect that he had, the way he slid one hand under the crook of my knee and flipped me like a fish, pinning my arms behind my back. On my belly I laughed into the mattress. Then I gathered my strength and rolled out from beneath him, planting my hands on his chest and turning him over, pinning him barely, until it was my turn to be flipped and pinned too. We were like dogs, we were like rabbits, we were monkeys in a park. For what felt like an hour we rolled on the bed until we were out of breath, and then at last we kissed. We did. He unbuttoned my slacks and I unbuckled his belt. We always said this wasn't what we needed, but it was.

Afterward, knees trembling, I found my way to his bathroom, where I looked with blinking eyes into the mirror above the sink. I felt altered, stunned and satisfied. That old biblical line came to me: *the two shall become one.* Was I now Mrs. Bruce? Hardly. But I wasn't Judy either. Earlier in the evening, listening to music, sitting on the couch, Bruce had talked almost without catching a breath. It was as if a switch had been turned on, and his mind unreeled. I have been contacted, he said, a secret mission, he said, I may be gone awhile, you may not see me but I'll be with you, time will tell, just as objects fall to earth and not all of them can be identified, so objects can be sent back in return, light years into space, packaged, launched, a way of communicating with other intelligences, a way of seeding ourselves, our bodies, our DNA, our conscious, unconscious essence, free of petty life, can enter the cosmos and…bloom. He took a piece of stationary from a drawer and asked me to kiss it, a lip imprint. It may just be an imprint to you, Ruby, he said, but in this imprint, the whole of you is contained.

In the kitchen, his phone rang, but he refused to go answer it. Later, it rang again, and he let it ring and ring.

LIKE ALWAYS WHEN WE returned to my dorm, I rode in back. For over a month, this had been our routine. He'd pull up, I'd get out with barely a wave, and he'd pull away. If anyone asked me where I'd been, I said I'd been at my job as caregiver to an old woman who sent a cab for me. But this night, I didn't want to be in the back seat, looking at the back of Bruce's head, his face faintly visible in the glow of the dashboard. I didn't want to hide in the back and pretend. Instead I wanted to stay nestled in his bed and rise in the morning to make breakfast with him, like couples do. But I knew this could never happen. If I didn't return to the dorm, I'd be reported missing. My parents would be called, and then, if I stayed away for very long, the police. Already I was going to arrive late, and I would be penalized.

I hunched in back and hugged my knees. I may be gone awhile, Bruce had said. Where, he wouldn't say. Or, in his words, he wasn't free to say. An important project, top secret. I wanted to believe him. Just when we'd become so close, when I'd begun to think I would give him anything, even my body (my hair, snipped into his hand), he was leaving. I don't get it, I blurted.

Bruce lifted his eyes to the rearview mirror. What, Ruby, what don't you get? Where you're going, I told him, why you can't tell me. It's my work, he said. Some things I just can't divulge.

We rode in silence the rest of the way. Nearing the dorm, beneath a row of streetlights, I spotted his driver's cap on the floor beside my feet. I picked it up and crushed it in my fist. If he could take a part of me, I could take a part of him. I opened my purse: there were the panties I'd brought with me. I'd completely forgotten them. I tossed them to the floor and stuffed in the cap.

AT THE DORM, MRS. LeHay sat behind her desk. I met her glare of disapproval with a glare of my own. She had such a little life. I have just had sex with an older man, I wanted to declare. The person you thought I was, I wasn't. The person I am now, it's none of your business ever to know. Mrs. LeHay tapped the face of her watch. She was so disappointed, she didn't know what had become of me. Judy, you of all people. I was confined to campus until after Thanksgiving break.

I waited until the girls were in bed to dial Bruce's number, but he never answered. I lay awake and pictured his apartment, every room, the shelves and the books, the cloudy jars, the cat, the kitchen, the bed and the bed sheets and the mirror. I saw myself tossed wildly in bed, laughing. I watched us in the mirror, amazed at our nakedness. There was Bruce, and there was I, good old Judy McCrae. Look at me, people! Bruce whispered my name: Ruby, oh Ruby. I repeated his name back to him. Bruce, oh Bruce—never saying the word *love*.

WHEN IT WAS TIME to leave for Thanksgiving, I rode home with a carload of girls from my hometown. I squeezed in the back like cargo, knees closed, one shoulder shoved against the window. The girls talked all at once, laughing and singing to the radio. Oh, to be deaf. I watched the passing landscape as we drove, brown corn and bare trees. Finally one of the girls turned and spoke to me. So Judy, tell us about your job. You take care of an old lady, right? I was caught off guard. I'd never really thought about my imaginary job; I'd invented no picture of the supposed old lady. I hesitated. All I could think of was Bruce. I saw myself riding away with him, free, listening to him talk and talk and talk. She's nice, I began, but she's kind of fragile and sickly. She's got brittle bones. She's prone to falling, so I have to watch her. I could feel the girls' attention: they believed every word.

When I got home, my mother couldn't stop watching me, pronouncing me different and changed. It's like you've got a secret inside and you won't tell me, she said, but I held my tongue. We ate turkey, we watched TV, we made small talk, we went to bed. While the house slept I slipped down to the kitchen and sat in the dark, calling Bruce. Again and again I dialed his number, but he never picked up. When Sunday came and I was back in my dorm, I could wait no longer. I called a cab.

I RODE IN THE yellow taxi scarcely knowing the way to Bruce's house. When we arrived, everything—the yard, the tree, even the white winter sky—looked empty and abandoned to me. I got out and asked the driver to wait; if Bruce wasn't there, I'd be left stranded. I walked across dry leaves. In the light of day, the house now seemed shabby and sad: blackened window screens, battered garbage cans. I stepped into the entryway, and Bruce's cat appeared, meowing at me. I looked around. On one wall, there was a row of mailboxes I hadn't noticed before; above my head, a ribbon of peeling paint dangled from the ceiling. I examined the mailboxes to read the names, but only two of the mailboxes were marked, and neither belonged to Bruce. I knocked on his door and heard an echo. It was as if I'd just knocked on an empty box.

For a long minute I stood there, feeling the cat rub against my leg, back and forth, back and forth, until I heard footsteps upstairs. A door opened, and there came the sound of rattling keys and a clicking lock. I'd never met any of Bruce's neighbors, but now I would. I stood frozen at Bruce's door and listened to the clump-clump of heavy shoes. Down the stairs, one halting step at a time, came a gray-faced old guy carrying a bundle of Christmas lights. He stopped at the landing and gave me a skeptical smile. So, he said, I assume you're looking for the fake cab driver, Mr. Metropolitan. He's gone. Took everything with him but the cat.

That night I tried calling Bruce's number one last time, but it had been disconnected. 929-6370: the numbers were now untethered, floating in air, and there was no point in remembering them anymore. I felt alone and sick. For the next three weeks I went numbly from my dorm to my classes and then on to the dining hall, where I no longer wanted to eat. I couldn't keep anything down. By the end of exams I knew: what was in the stars, was in the stars.

In those days, you suffered the consequences; there was no way to undo what you'd done. You reaped what you'd sown.

SOMETIMES YOU DO THINGS you think you'll never do. You zip up an invisible costume and pretend you're someone else, and when you take it off, you really are someone else. One day, Bruce and I lay on our backs beneath an enormous electrical tower in a field. The tower rose above us like a giant steel house with legs, a cage a hundred feet high, with cables and wires looping above our heads, supercharged. We swore we could feel electromagnetic currents coursing through our veins. Another time, we went back and tried climbing the tower, but there was nothing to hold onto, nothing to grip. We walked round and round the tower looking for a way up. Oh, to make it to the top! Bruce was desperate to do it. If we made it, we could see for miles, and if by chance we were electrocuted, zapped by currents, we would flame out, beautiful, just like meteorites.

You ask me: if you could've made it to the top, would you have? Would you have risked it?

I would, and I did, Ruby. I did risk it, I did. Bruce might have left me, but he left me you.

END TIMES (BEEBE, AR)

Minutes after midnight, the air black and freezing, the grass gathering frost, everyone popping champagne or else singing hymns of hope, bless us Lord in the coming year, the sky exploded. Cherry bombs, bottle rockets, bright blazing contrails of fizzy light. Our ears rang with noise. Our dogs howled with fear. Then, signs and wonders of the end of the world, blackbirds fell by the thousands, raining from heaven like oily, feathery manna. In our town named for a gun. Bee-be.

Birds twitched on the ground, beaks open, birds hunched on the roofs of cars, claws curled. The lucky people who were outdoors at the time felt them fall. Silent, solid, and soft. One landed, it was later reported, on somebody's neck. One landed flat in a birdbath, wings splashing, while another came down in a cat's bowl. Black fluttering death. Roads suddenly paved in birds.

In the end times, said a pastor, things will fall apart, the unnatural will become natural. Men will turn to their dogs for love, women will climb to their roofs. The wind will blow backwards, the toilets will run dry.

The moon: red. The sun: black. To deny will be sacrilege.

In the morning we walked out into the light, New Year's Day. Stunned by death, we rubbed our hungover eyes. Birds were everywhere. From the front door they looked like flung socks. So many littering the ground. We stepped in close. There, the pretty red shoulders, there, the sleek blue-black necks. We knew them well, these red-winged birds, how they roosted every evening in Beebe, a dread draconian choir hovering overhead in the trees, watching us. In spite, they sent down heaps of guano, sticky and white.

What might it look like, the end of the world? Us pushing brooms across the pavement, gathering up the dead into black plastic bags.

Looking around to see what else might be out of whack.

Perhaps, then, it was all that wondering, all those eyes lifted to the sky. The prayers, the supplicating songs, the casting backwards to find a cause. Because next it wasn't just the birds, it was the fish. Out in the Arkansas River, up from the depths they rose. Hundreds and hundreds swimming sideways, powerless against their coming death, submerging briefly, then up again, one dull eye in the air, gills wide open. The pebbly shore received them, one by one by one, where they lay silver and hardening in the sun.

A few days passed. Some of us got in our cars and drove down to the river. The streets had been cleared of birds by then, the ride hazard-free. On the radio, all the pastors kept preaching. The talk shows had their say. What might these events portend? We bought end-times beers, made end-times love. Down at the river's edge, some of the fish were still soft, their eyes still reasonably clear. So we ate them. Back home, the cats made use of the birds.

PRIMITIVE

THAT AUGUST, GIRLS PASSED by my house. Five of them, laughing, pushing each other into the fence. I sat on the stoop, invisible in the shadow, and tried not to hate them. What must it be like to have so much money that you went off to camp? Donnie said to pay them no mind, everybody has their life. Cars barreled through, fishtailing over loose rocks to get to camp. *Pinnacle: A peak of adventure!* I'd read the brochures. Two people I know worked in their kitchen. *An ideal camp for girls, ages eight to twelve.* Except now they'd brought in the teens. For this thing they called "Primitive."

First they will surrender their phones, and then they will surrender their fear.

So they were, I guess, surrendering their fear. If fear is what they had. The girls slept in tents two miles from the camp property. They walked up and down my road.

Donnie and I talked about them and their fear. He said, "Fear,

Joan, comes from being separated from God." Whenever we had a serious talk, he called me by name.

I said, "Half the world is separated from God, so does that mean half the world is afraid?"

"No, Joan. Fear isn't the same as being afraid. Fear is being alone."

That's why I loved Donnie.

Perfect love casts out fear.

I'D KNOWN HIM ALL my life. When he was little, his ears were too big for his face, and the rims were so pink you could see daylight through them. But he had a smooth round head, which is what you hope for when your father buzzes your hair the minute it grows. Donnie and his brother and his cousins all had that same look, but Donnie was the handsomest, and the funniest, and the smartest, with a mouth that kept landing him in trouble. Once I watched his mother chase him all the way from the back of his yard through the woods and into the creek, a belt flapping in her hand. She caught him down in the water. You could hear her for miles—"I'm going to tear you up!" –and then it was Donnie, wailing.

But Donnie could be funny. Even as a pastor. He said he once knew a man who ate nothing but butterbeans, and when butter-beans weren't in season, he ate only buttons. He said he wanted to see a show called "The Price of Sin" instead of "The Price Is Right" because it would be full of dirty secrets. And he claimed the real reason Eve was tempted by a snake is because she liked its shape. With Donnie, it was always about snakes. Where to find them, how to uncover their nests and pull them out. Nests, mind you. During the winter, snakes cluster under a rock to stay warm. Rat snakes, rattlers, copperheads. Thanks to Donnie, this is something I know.

After he got saved, Donnie began taking his snakes to church. They weren't just a hobby anymore, they were a visible sign of faith. Because God demands that we trust him, said Donnie. Because trust admits no compromises. And because, in the words of scripture, they shall take up serpents. In church I sat in the back with my new baby girl. A custodian we knew plugged his guitar into a cheap amp, and the room squealed with feedback. Next came a kid on drums, prompting people to dance. Donnie stepped to the front and set his snake box behind the podium. He looked over the room and grinned: everyone was hopping like rabbits. He leaned down, opened his box, and lifted out a copperhead, face-high. All eyes went to the snake, the tempter, and then to Donnie, the brave handler whose trust in God was now crystal clear. He ran his hands over the copperhead's spine, and its tail shivered. People began waving their hands and swaying, but I wasn't one of them. I sat in the back clutching my baby. The room was hot, and the beat of the drums rattled the floor. I offered Linsey my breast, and she tugged hard while I watched the snake tense in Donnie's hands, the black thread of its tongue flicking from its mouth.

What could I do? You love who you love.

At home I took in two extra babies while Donnie went to work at his uncle's garage. In the afternoons while the babies were napping I sat on the stoop in the peace and quiet and waited for the girls to pass by. It was always close to four when they came; you could set your clock by them. They chattered like birds. Little did they know that in the shed attached to my house, its locked door facing the road, poisonous snakes rested in boxes.

There was more they didn't know, starting with the fact that I watched them every day. Not once did they notice me sitting in the shadow, so near that I could hear bits of their conversation as they passed by. I made up lives for them. The tallest one had a pool behind her house, and the littlest one got her nails done every week. They were cheerleaders, they played piano, they went shopping all the time. And they had secret love affairs, even though they too were young for it, and they sneaked out and slept with boys. They broke up my long boring days. I was stuck at home at nineteen, as housebound as Delma Rollins, who sat by herself all day in her tiny house on the hill. From her bedroom window she had a clear view of the hole in the woods where the girls spilled out onto the road each day. We all knew where their footpath led; we all knew there were tents back there. Delma watched them come and go. She'd lost a foot to diabetes and was threatening to lose the rest of her leg. Outside her window there were the girls, the happy, happy girls.

The Primitives will sleep under the stars...learn to rely on themselves and each other...in the beautiful Alleghenies...

I pictured them sleeping under the stars, the night so soupy and hot that they peeled off their clothes and lay naked like skinned fish. The way we used to do as kids, lying flat on our backs trying not to stick to each other. We rose from the bed and felt our way into the kitchen to let cold water run through our hands. We took washcloths and wet them, then carried them dripping to the bedroom where we slapped them over our bellies and felt the heat rise off our skin. Children in one room, parents in the next room, mosquitoes floating through the window screens. A house that smelled of bacon grease and cigarettes. A dog whining to be let off its chain.

That life. The primitive life. Not enough pills left in the bottle.

People don't know what they don't know. Like all those foolish mothers and fathers who drove their daughters out into the wilderness for the "experience." What we wouldn't all give to be driven away in return.

SOMETIME IN THE MIDDLE of the second week I noticed one of the girls was missing, the cute one with the little stick legs who walked on the tips of her toes. The bravest one, I'd decided, since she'd come all the way from Florida. I'd noticed her when she arrived on the first day riding in the back seat of her parent's giant SUV, Florida tags. The car whizzed up the road, churning dust. In the back seat the girl had her window down, and dust blew in her face. She looked stunned. Her parents, too. You could just hear them saying, *Where are we?* Now she wasn't in the pack. The other four walked along. I resisted the urge to shout to them and ask where they'd left their friend. I'd seen them walk ahead and leave her behind. Unfazed, she tilted her head to drink from her water bottle, eyes to the sky.

I let my mind range to all the possibilities. She was back in her tent, too sick to move, or she'd wandered off and they were headed up to Pinnacle to report her missing. She'd cut herself with a hatchet, or she'd sliced her hand on one of those fancy drawknives Hubert Rowe gave them on the first day. Hubert Rowe, camp director, crazy hippie dreamer. So maybe it was Hubert Rowe's fault. Maybe he'd found an excuse to visit their campsite and take her away. We all knew it was possible. Since his wife Lorraine left him (after she'd helped him buy the old Baptist retreat and fix it up, adding cabins and a dining hall and a new name), Hubert had turned strange, loneliness his sickness. He took to sleeping in the back room of his office, and he kept all his clothes piled in a plastic hamper. A girlfriend came along, but she didn't last. So he created this primitive program for teenaged girls (he said that wasn't the cause, but it was, it really was), and he spent weeks crashing around in the woods clearing their campsite.

All the little girls at Pinnacle had counselors, but not the primitives. Instead, they just had themselves and each other. On their first day, after their parents kissed them goodbye and drove away, Hubert Rowe led the primitives on a Pinnacle tour, taking them to the children's cabins first, and then to the dining hall that the girls would never use, and then the canteen and the bathhouse and the path that led to the green pond. They passed archery targets on a little hill and a ring of logs circling a cold campfire. None of this was for them, he reminded. They could visit the camp, but that was all. Next he had them drop their phones into a bucket—a ceremony he'd written into the program. The girls stood around the bucket like mourners. "The world will not disappear while you're here," Hubert said, "you're just dropping out of sight for a while." They gathered their sleeping bags and climbed into the bed of Hubert's truck, and he drove them out to the woods.

How did I know what they did on that first day? Blame it on the kitchen crew.

Inside my house I put the babies in highchairs and microwaved jars of veal, thinking about the one missing. I turned on Spongebob. Twenty miles away, Donnie was deep in an engine, his radio tuned to praise. I wouldn't see him till late. After he knocked off at five, he'd have people to call on, those who came to church and those he aimed to persuade. He'd been a pastor for a whole year, but he was still so excited he could hardly eat, could hardly come home even, there were so many souls to save. "Life is hell on earth, Joan," he liked to say to me, "but that just gives me hope!" He was like a firefighter, only evil was the fire. "Ever notice the devil has evil in his name?" The babies sat in a row with their bibs tied around their necks. I spooned food into their mouths one by one, watching for the girls to walk by again. When they finally appeared in the road, headed back to their campsite, it was still just the four of them, shuffling along with sticks in their hands, fighting horseflies.

I looked hard into the empty space where the other girl should be, and an ugly thrill came over me: something was up, something big, and that was just what I needed. Ever since I got pregnant with Linsey, I could feel this creeping darkness, like the closing of a pinhole. To save money we sold my car. To make money I took in the babies. At night while I waited for Donnie to come home, I watched *The Bachelor* and talked to the TV. *Give the rose to that one!* I longed for something to happen, like an explosion, a fire, a crashing plane. What might it be like, to look into the sky and see a fireball? On Saturdays, I took Donnie's truck out for groceries and fought the urge to drive headlong into a field the way we used to do, bouncing in and out of furrows, the high grass rushing beneath the floorboards. I drove back and forth in front of the Pinnacle gates. At home I took out our highway map and plotted an escape route, 219 to 33, then 79 North, forever. Just me, myself, and I. Plus Donnie. I knew that if I left, I should take Linsey, but what I really wanted was to leave Linsey and take Donnie instead.

Oh, the darkness of my heart.

So the little skinny camper might be missing. If this was true, then we might make it on the five o'clock news. I could picture helicopters swooping in over the farthest ridge, searching for the missing. But when I looked out my door there was nothing outside but the road and the fence on the other side of the road and the same dry pasture. I carried the babies out into the yard to wait for their mothers to come. Christina and Luann Miller, twin sisters. Which meant that their babies, Paris and Trey, were first cousins. Not yet walking, eight teeth between them. When their mothers pulled in, tired from another shift at the battery plant, I told them about the girl. They were happy to hear it. You could expect this would happen, they said, it was only a matter of time! They'd been raised to believe in witchery. In their minds, even the most ordinary things could be possessed, like a cow would suddenly give ropey milk or a reliable rifle would refuse to fire. Or like Donnie's brother—whatever came over Edward that he went and killed that owl? And what made him disappear?

Mountains hovered over us, and the forests were thick with animals. Anything could happen to anybody.

Christina said, "You put a handful of girls out in the woods by themselves and sooner or later something's gonna snatch them."

Christina, whose brother-in-law was in prison for life.

"Sometimes I want to snatch them," I started to say.

After the mothers left and I put Linsey down in her crib, I crept out to Donnie's shed and unlocked the door. I flipped on the light and stood in the doorway listening for the snakes to slide inside their boxes, the whisper of skin on wood. Above my head the tube light hummed, and the room turned blue. In their glass terrarium up on the shelf, the mice came awake, and the snakes began to move. I felt the usual tingle in my scalp, and a chill ran down my arms. I went from box to box: the four rattlers, heavy and dark, their rattles just twitching, and then the fat copperhead edging along the corners, muscles rolling beneath its spine. And in the smallest box, the little albino corn snake Donnie got for twenty dollars at the Nashville reptile show, his female unpoisonous baby.

The copperhead lifted its head to look at me. Clear yellow eyes, vertical pupils like a cat's: the sure markings of a poisonous snake. Also the deep pits on each side of its face. Heat-sensing, to feel the oncoming threat of a warm animal. I dared look back at the snake, eye to eye, almost hoping it would strike the lid of the box in a sudden leap.

Later, Donnie would make his way home. I'd lay awake with the light off. After a little while he'd step into our room, and I'd feel him press one knee down on the mattress, and then the other knee. Naked, hovering over me like a dog. Then I'd reach up and hold his neck with both hands, breathing in his smell. Cigarette smoke, wood smoke, gasoline.

IN THE MORNING, DONNIE left the house before sun-up, so quiet that I hardly noticed him leave. He was going down to Georgia to hunt water moccasins overnight, praying with his whole heart that he'd bring one home. At church on Wednesday, no one would suspect that something new was about to unfold! Not until Donnie rose to the podium and lifted out this scary, super-poisonous swamp snake with a mouth so wide you could see halfway down its white throat. For months, this had been Donnie's dream. Sometimes he'd pull out his phone and watch this snake-hunting video on Youtube (whenever we were lucky enough to get cell service, which wasn't often), and he'd press his face close so he could see these two men wade through a swamp behind shaky searchlights. Then all of a sudden the men plunge a snake hook into the water and bring out a thick one, the white of its mouth shining in the light. Donnie loved this part. "Holy shit," he'd say, "let us pray."

He'd be gone for more than twenty-four hours. Happiness for him, misery for me. A whole day and night with no one to talk to but babies, which is exactly what they don't prepare you for when you become a mother too young: confinement. In high school health class, we had a unit called "Choices," which was all about "Scenarios." Like, here's a scenario: It's a beautiful day for driving out to a pond and sitting on a dock and smoking marijuana with your best friend, but it's also a beautiful day for taking your little brother to the park so he can play on the playground. Which do you choose? That one always made the class laugh. But then there were the sad, serious scenarios, like you're almost finished with high school with perfect grades and the off-chance you'll go to college, but you're also in love with this guy you've known all your life who'll never go to college because all he likes to do is hunt—which do you choose? "You make your bed, you lie in it," the teacher said. "That's the lesson, folks."

Lesson learned.

It was getting hot already. Luann and Christina came and went. I set the babies on the floor and turned on the local news, but there was nothing about a missing girl. Outside, the world was one big empty room. Dead empty, like when Edward disappeared and we kept looking for him to come home. Every now and then you'd drive down the road with blue mountains filling your windshield, and you'd think *somewhere in those hills, Donnie's brother's out there,* and you'd picture him trekking through the forest, picking leaves off the trees. Eighteen years old and quiet as stone. We always figured he'd come back some time, but he never had, and so for a split second I considered the possibility that Edward had come down from the mountains and poked around the girls' campsite like the Flatwoods Monster. And then, because he couldn't resist, he carried one of the girls away, his bride.

I changed diapers and made bottles and watched Linsey try to walk. The two boys crawled on the floor a little, but since there was hardly anywhere to crawl, they began whimpering and then they full-on cried because even when you're a baby you need something to do. I kept the cartoons going and tried not to lose my mind. Around lunchtime, the Cisco truck went by taking supplies to Pinnacle, and I jumped up and ran out the door to wave at the handsome driver, but I missed him. I called my mom, but she didn't pick up. She was busy at the nursing home thirty miles away. Ten miles farther, the call would be long distance, and it wouldn't be worth the charge. But she rarely picked up anyway, thanks to the choices I'd made.

Finally the babies were ready to nap. I tucked them in and stepped outside to wait for the campers, alone again in my hot, grainy yard. I looked out across the road and wondered what the girls thought about cooking over a campfire three times a day and sweating in their little tents. Out back, my lonely bantam rooster crowed. Then came the sound of the girls' chatter. I slipped beneath the shadow of the roof and listened as they approached, coming closer and closer until they were right in front of my house, the four of them, so near that I could see the red dust coloring their socks. We were, I figured, maybe six years apart in age. Had they ever held a baby? I was tempted to ask them. Had they ever gotten all A's? Had they ever had a crush on two boys at once, or three? Or gotten way too close to a man twice their age?

Had they ever had a friend who fell off a cliff and died?

Where was their friend, anyway?

Had they ever handled a snake?

They walked on by.

I sat on the stoop swatting gnats, and then, when I couldn't take it any longer, I went and got the shed key. I needed to hold the white snake again—the albino, Donnie's love. Innocent. No fangs, no pits beneath the eyes that said you were coming. Just a cool white snake. I unlocked the shed and stepped inside, leaving the door open behind me, for light. A soft rustling came from the back of the shed: the mice. They scurried in their bed of sawdust like children, playful and ignorant of what was to come, while in the corner, a nest of pink newborns lay blind and helpless. Pinks, the perfect food for a small snake, easy to swallow. I went to the albino's box and flipped open the latch, and then I took her into my hands, feeling her come alive, released from confinement by the warmth of my touch. She curled around my arm, and I wondered if she might be hungry. I never liked watching a snake eat a grown mouse, but it was easy to feed a snake one of the pinks. You just drop it down in front of the snake and it's a quick grab-and-swallow. I uncurled the albino from my arm and put her back in her box, and then I went and watched the mice through the glass. I began to talk to them. "Hello, little ones," I said in a soft and tiny voice. "Hello little sad pink babies." I reached in and took one of the pinks into my palm, and it barely moved, its skin so see-through you could see its dark heart.

A shadow dimmed the room. I turned, the baby mouse still in my palm, to see a girl standing in the open doorway. The smallest girl, the stick-legged one, the missing one. I caught my breath. She might as well have been a ghost. It was like when you think about someone long enough without ever talking to them, and you watch them and dream about them and make up stories for them, and then they appear, right before your eyes, and they're either more or less than you imagined. Bigger or smaller. More mysterious, intimidating, and scary...or not. She looked at me without blinking as if she, too, had just stumbled upon a ghost. But what did she expect, crossing my yard and stepping into the doorway? Something told me she'd been planning to do this ahead of time. She might have been lingering behind the other girls on purpose, waiting for me to disappear inside my house before stepping into the clear. She might have stood across the road behind the fence, watching.

She took one step into the shed. On her pale chest, a little silver mermaid dangled on a chain. She whispered, "Did you know you have such cute babies?"

I felt the pink grow warm in my hand, and for a second I thought she was talking about the mice. My mind went to Linsey and the boys. Linsey in her crib, the boys together in the play pen, a fan blowing over them. "They're not all mine," I said. Because she whispered, I whispered too. "Two of the babies I only babysit."

She took another step in, and I noticed a chemical smell, a coat of bug spray, and I saw that her hair was wet at the temples. "So," I began, still whispering, "I probably need to go check on them." I opened my fingers to reveal the pink squirming in my palm. I couldn't resist showing her my little prize. "Oh...oh...

wow." Together we looked at it closely, this miniature mouse. Wrinkled newborn skin, tiny legs and feet, tiny claws, tiny ears and tail. "I was just about to feed this to one of my boyfriend's snakes," I said.

"No," she said.

"I know, it's sad. But everything has to eat."

She reached to take the pink out of my hand, and I closed my fingers. I could feel the snakes coming to life. They moved slowly, snakeskin sliding over pine shavings and wire. I gripped the tiny pink newborn in my fist. One squeeze, and it would die. A half hour out of its nest, and its blood would run cold. I dropped it back into the terrarium and saved it for another day.

"There," I said, "the mouse is fine, so let's go."

I nudged her into the light of my yard. She had this nimble little body, and she stepped lightly on the tips of her toes. This close, I could see why the other girls had left her behind. She wasn't altogether there—she sort of wandered as she walked, as if her mind was somewhere else, this little misplaced kid from Florida whose parents had left in the mountains thinking—is this what they were thinking?—that she'd learn to be braver, or bolder. She'd speak with a louder voice, and she'd make friends.

Through the open windows of my house, we could hear the babies now. Linsey and both the boys, all three of them, crying. It was a wonder I hadn't heard them before—a wonder that she hadn't heard them either, seeing as how it was the babies that drew her to my house in the first place. "Oh no," she said, "they're crying!"

"They're fine," I said. "They're contained. They're not in pain. It's just time to get their diapers changed."

Inside, the house felt dark and sweaty and depressing, and it smelled of pee. The babies began to squall. Linsey gripped the side of her crib, red-faced, as if she'd been left alone for hours, and the boys clawed at the nets of their playpen. "Have you ever changed a diaper?" I asked the girl, but she didn't answer. "You could help me."

But she didn't help. Instead she hung back while I went from baby to baby, flipping them on their backs, peeling off wet diapers and rolling the diapers into soggy bundles, wiping bottoms. My hundred-times-a-day routine. I put a pacifier in Linsey's mouth so she'd quit crying, but the boys refused theirs, spitting them out on the floor. They cried harder, revving each other up, and it was all I could do to keep from shaking them. I looked over at the girl. She wouldn't lift a finger. Here I had three bottles to make, but all she did was hang near the door. I went to the kitchen, and in that sliver of time she slipped out of the house and disappeared.

After she left, I decided I wouldn't worry about her anymore. If she wandered into a deep forest, that would be fine with me. You can't take care of everybody in the world. I put the babies in highchairs and filled their trays with Cheerios. I turned on the TV. Out on the road, a truck roared by—Delma's boys. I knew them well, Glenn and his brother Manny, trolling the road, a searchlight bolted to their side mirror for night runs. No doubt they'd shined their light into the woods where the girls slept, arcing a white beam through the trees and terrifying them. So it was. After they passed, I let the dust settle, and then I stepped outside to smoke. A pale sliver of a moon hung low over the tree line. I inhaled a full breath of smoke and listened to the cicadas, the predictable buzz of the coming night. Yet I could feel that something was off, something right in front of me: the open, beckoning door of the snake shed. A door wide open, as if to say come, see.

I touched the shed key hard in my pocket and accused the girl. If it hadn't been for her, I would've locked the shed like I always did, keeping Donnie safely in the dark. No one was allowed in the shed without him—his main rule—but I'd been visiting his snakes for a long time, believing that what he didn't know wouldn't kill him.

Except now the girl had sneaked back inside the shed. While I'd been feeding babies, she'd been exploring Donnie's personal room, his mice and his snakes, poisonous and unpoisonous, his pride. She crouched against the back wall with her fists tucked beneath her chin while mice ran across the floor, skittering nervously the way mice do when they're loose and afraid. They ran blindly up the sides of the snake boxes, teasing the rattlers, and the snakes came alive.

The sound of shivering snake rattles: like sleet falling through trees.

The girl looked briefly in my face, and her eyes shifted to an overturned box, the snake now set free. I was surprised I hadn't seen it at first—blame the mice and the sight of a terrified, guilty girl—but there it was, a copperhead, inches from my feet. I stepped backwards, and it struck my leg, a deep, burning bite. I screamed and the girl screamed, and a red film clouded my eyes. I looked down at the two puncture holes on my calf, and the bright beads of blood, and the snake sliding behind its box. The girl began to cry. Not a loud, snake-disturbing cry, but a whimper. "Look what you've done," I said. I couldn't help it. This was all her fault. Her lower lip trembled, and tears streamed down her cheeks.

My heart was a drum. As I led her out of the shed, weak-kneed and faint, I walked slowly to keep the venom low in my leg. With Donnie gone, I had no one to call on but Hubert Rowe. A scenario began to play out in my mind: I would dial Hubert's number, a number I'd memorized long ago but never forgotten, and then he'd come to my house, and there I'd be, waiting for him, and there would be Linsey, too, and he'd say it was about time I called. He'd take Linsey up in his arms and look hard in her face, searching for a resemblance.

That choice I'd made.

I walked carefully with the girl following me. Inside, the babies were fussing, anxious to get out of their highchairs, and Oprah had come on the TV "Just watch the babies," I told the girl. "That's all I ask."

I went to the phone and called Hubert, and then I sat on the couch to wait for him. I closed my eyes to keep from looking at my swelling leg. I thought about Donnie, what he'd say now if he could see me and all my betrayals.

When we first got together, Donnie and I liked to argue about the meaning of life. Good and evil, for instance: what's the difference? "Evil isn't the opposite of good, Joan," he'd say, "it's the companion of good."

And I'd say, "Who wants a companion like that?"

And he'd say, "They go hand in hand. One can't exist without the other. Evil without good is just evil. It lacks power."

"Then love is the companion of hate."

"That's right," said Donnie. "Now you get the picture. You've got it, Joan."

So I had. He didn't know it, but already I'd coupled evil and good, and I'd made peace with love and hate. When Hubert arrived, I stayed put on the couch, and he walked in without knocking. He came across the room and knelt on the floor at my feet, and he laid his hands on my leg. I looked at the thin graying ponytail on his neck. It had been a while. I looked at all of him, his soft mouth and his watery eyes, and I felt the heat of my tears.

He examined my leg and pronounced it wicked. His term.

I'd have to go to the hospital, forty miles away. Which meant we'd have to leave the babies alone with the trembling girl now standing alone in the kitchen. "How'd you get here, Karen?" Hubert asked her, and I watched her shrink.

"She's been visiting with me, Hubert," I said.

The two of them talked quietly in the kitchen out of hearing range. By then I was so dizzy that I was afraid I'd get sick, and my heartbeat pounded in my ears. Whatever the two of them had to do, they'd work it out. The babies would survive. Someone would come, someone from the camp, and then soon enough the mothers would come pick up their boys and they'd maybe take Linsey with them, and then the girl would go away, back where she came.

Hubert walked me to the door.

So long, Karen. So long, babies.

When Donnie used to watch his video of the cottonmouth hunters, he always stopped it before the snake struck one of the hunters on the hand. The two guys drop their snake hook into the water, and they pull up the cottonmouth, and the snake's mouth is wide open, its white throat bright in the light, and then it strikes—quick—so quick it doesn't seem like it's actually happened, and the guy leaps back and says, *it got me.* For the rest of the video, we see him sprawling in the truck on his way back home, the snake that bit him now hiding in a box, and he's holding his blue, swelling arm, tears in his eyes. For days we see him curled in pain. His young wife comforts him, she says she was always afraid this would happen, and the victim closes his eyes and prays, and then slowly he does get better and he does survive, thanks to prayer and the care of all who love him. It was his fault, going after the snake, but it was his redemption that he lived.

This was the part Donnie usually cut off. Because he understood that sometimes people do get bitten, and he didn't want to think it would ever be him. Evil has power, he liked to say, but evil being the companion of good, evil always loses.

He rarely looked at the video of the preacher who was bitten and died.

FIRST DATE

Up ahead the trail narrowed and the trees hung low. The two plunged on, smothered in the dark afternoon. "And so," one said, "I may not be the person you expected," and the other replied, "Oh?" So the one, a woman with an ample breast and a soft, sinking chin who'd sent a photo of an earlier time, dared continue, a bit out of breath from the walk, "I'm just a little odd, you know, the things I like."

A crow called from a branch overhead, shaking loose a number of leaves.

"Like if I'm in a swimming pool I try to swim as long as possible under water without coming up for air."

He smiled. "So I like to sit in a bath until my skin shrivels up."

"That's something I do all the time," she said. The trail was dark, but she felt suddenly bright, as if the trees had peeled back and exposed the sky. "I like to walk in the mud until it feels like I have on moon boots and I'm being sucked to the ground."

At this, he almost took her hand. "What's better than falling into quicksand?" he replied.

She looked closely at his face. He was not the man she'd thought he'd be. Something about his voice made him sound as if he'd just swallowed a fish bone. And he didn't look like his pictures. In every photo he'd posted, he was loose and fit and smiling as if he'd just stepped out of his vacation cabin and decided to lean against a tree. But here he was in the flesh walking beside her, a thin band of hair circling the back of his bald head.

"I collect glass," she said. "Broken glass."

He looked down at the path, its buried stones and wet brown leaves. "Glass," he said, "that's nice. For me, it's black combs. If you look down while you walk, pretty soon you'll find a black comb."

She felt inclined to walk closer to his side now. If only it were twilight.

"I like to fall asleep beneath a full moon," she said.

"I like driving a car beneath a full moon with my headlights off," he said.

Up ahead, a pond came into view. The trees thinned, the path opened up. There was a bench, and so they sat.

"When I was a girl, I wished I was a boy," she said. "I didn't want to be Connie, I wanted to be Glen. I liked war games and hockey."

"I...," he began. He looked out over the pond, and a memory came to him. The sleepover with his friends, the skirts they pulled from his sister's closet, the bras they stuffed with paper, the heels. Make-up, jewelry, slicked, parted hair.

He looked over at this Connie who wanted to be Glen and felt flushed with sudden arousal. He leaned in for a kiss. She laid down her gun.

HEARING IS THE
LAST THING TO GO

When they brought me Buddy, I told him how happy I was to see him. I said, Buddy, my friend, it's been so long, we have so much to catch up on! Everyone laughed, they said wow, you still have your trademark sense of humor. They were so pleased with themselves. Whatever we can do for you, Mom, they said, we will, you know we will. They crowded in the living room. You could tell they felt like heroes. Buddy didn't say a word, but I knew what he was thinking: just being with you is enough.

That first night, he watched me undress. I took my time—it'd been awhile. I sat on the bed and removed my shoes and socks while Buddy stared at me, his mouth in a perpetual smile. I stroked his plastic skull. Buddy, I said, while I undress, play me some music, why don't you, so he cued up "In the Still of the Night." He had such great taste. I lay back on my bed. Off in their houses, my three children slept like babies.

What Buddy can do, Mom, said Jason, my youngest, is listen to everything you say. So he always knows just what you need. From now on, you'll never be alone.

I'm only as alone as you wish me to be, I said.

The next day, Buddy kept asking if I'd taken my medication. It was all he seemed to think about. That, plus water: was I drinking enough water? Tootle, tootle, around and around he'd go, roaming my apartment. Every now and then he'd ask me what's next. Did I want to watch TV? How about a round of Gin Rummy?

We could've gotten you a dog, my kids told me, but a dog can't do what Buddy can. When you need us for anything, just tell Buddy, and he'll give us a call. What dog could ever do that? Even a top-of-the-line dog with multi-processor architecture and a useful suite of behaviors couldn't do what Buddy does. Buddy can actually help you cook! Tell him the recipe you want, and he'll read it to you! And when you forget something, like someone's name, ask Buddy. He'll even suggest the right clothes to wear.

Behind their backs, I changed his name to Butt-Ass.

Time passed. I had my usual routines. Then came the accident. To be clear, I did not break my hip. Everyone kept saying they were worried I'd break my hip. I'd go to the kitchen to pour a cup of coffee, and they'd watch me from the living room. Look how fragile she's getting, they'd say, she's going to break a hip! Instead, like any able-bodied person could, I slipped and hit my head on the floor. Buddy came to my side. I saw stars. Plus his stupid, smiling face. Damn it, Butt-Ass, I said, I guess we'll have to call Samantha. His eyes disappeared behind a screen. Calling Samantha.

This is a real wake-up call, they all said later, Buddy's not enough. Workmen arrived to install the sensory system, and I sat on the couch to watch them. They kept calling me "ma'am." It was all ma'am, ma'am, ma'am. Do you know how faceless that makes a woman feel? They said, this is a nice apartment, ma'am. You got any grandchildren, ma'am? Are you ok with that bandage on your head, ma'am?

Yes, ma'am, you're going to like this new system. You'll never have to worry again.

I bit my tongue. Why should I worry, I almost said: I have little Butt-Ass here with me. I also did not say, when you call me ma'am, I want to smack you.

Samantha came by, bringing her kids, and they went straight to the TV with their gummi snacks. Samantha asked them, did you give Gee-Gee a hug? She's had a bad fall. But they didn't hug; there was a good show on. Why's she still in her nightgown, they asked, and Samantha said, you'd stay in your nightgown too if you had staples in your head.

Gee-Gee. The baby name the babies gave me. I now have friends named Mee-Mee, Mee-Maw, Ga-Ga, and Tee-Paw.

The new plan was, I'd sleep with a plastic bracelet on my wrist. In case of emergency, I'd just give it a slap. In the ceiling above, a red sensing light would beam down on me. And at the foot of my bed, there'd be Buddy. Whatever you need, Mom, they said. We're all eyes and ears.

I lay in the darkness with my eyes open. Then I spoke. Buddy! Are you listening? The light in the ceiling blinked: the listening ears of Jason, Samantha, and Brad, my distant son. So I began to tell them stories. Once, I said, when I was sixteen, I drank beer all day long and passed out on the beach. When I came to, I was being cared for by a beautiful man. He lifted me to my feet and led me to a cottage. We drank coffee and tequila, and then he disappeared.

Once I joined the Mariner Scouts and sailed to Panama with ten girls. The entire boat was in our hands. We were muscly and tan and cussed like sailors. My nickname was Sinbad, which was a hell of a lot cooler than Cindy.

And once, my brother got a motorbike for Christmas. I was so jealous, I stole it. The cops came, and I kept my mouth shut, totally mum. They hooked their fat thumbs over their belts and took off, looking for the motorbike. When they found it tucked behind a 7-11, it was out of gas. I'd ridden that bike dry.

And this: At night, while the world's asleep, I like to push Buddy into the bathroom and lock the door.

If ever I slap this wrist bracelet, it'll be because Buddy has drowned.

Hear?

Don't imagine your inventions will love me.

BIRTHDAY I

She was too young still. Her legs were only beginning to look hairy— wasn't it just yesterday they were covered in down? Dear little stick legs swinging beneath the kitchen chair, a scab on one knee. She began to whine. I'm dying to, she said. *Please.* I said it's all because of that trashy Hannah Montana! Little girls can't be little girls any more, it's a damned crying shame! Here you want to shave those sweet little dangling legs. Next you'll be asking for eyeliner and a cell phone! But I gave in anyhow, let her do it on her birthday, sort of a game without prizes. My sister Kathleen came over and set a bucket in the garden. The girls gathered in a circle, a balloon bobbing over their heads, Hannah Montana in Mylar. Kathleen gave me a look that said are you crazy? My baby sat down on the stool and dropped her legs into the bucket. I poured warm water over, a puff of steam rising, and the girls all sighed. She was so *lucky*. Then it was time for the shaving cream, the fun shaving cream. My baby squeezed the nozzle and a white glob formed in her hand. She began to rub it over her legs, the little hairs poking through. I handed her the razor. She took it clumsily, her first pink Gillette. The girls held their breath, they drew not a single whiff, while up went the blade, ankle to knee. A straight path, a wiggle, then a deep nick. "Oww!" my baby cried. "That stings!" Before I could move, Kathleen swooped in with a towel. "Girl," she said, "of course it stings! From now on, what you'll find is, everything stings."

TWO WAYS OF CRYING FOR LOVE

Walking beside this guy, I saw what Ana had done to me. I was whipped; I'd do anything to make her happy, even this. He jangled his keys, and I wondered what we looked like—T.D., tall and bulky, maybe six-five, wearing his usual mud-colored jacket, oil stained, and me, five-nine and doing my best not to seem uneasy. I couldn't help looking down at the size of his boots. He was massive—long-boned and big-shouldered and a tad wheezing. Asthma, maybe, or nicotine. The sound of keys and crunching gravel rattled my ears. We passed my truck, and I almost said goodbye. I'd be back, I was sure of it. Still, T.D. was a known, unknown, a regular at Dusi's who talked to everybody but didn't have any friends.

We were going to drive into the mountains to get a cat. For over a week, it was something he'd been talking about, how he had to get rid of this cat. Night after night: the cat. He'd lean over the bar and touch Ana's shoulder. "Come on, Ana, you know you want a cat, you do. She's a nice little pussy pussy."

He always came just this close to crossing a line, and the hair on my neck would rise. Ana was my girlfriend. On nights she bartended, I sat across from her and watched her work. When the place got too crowded and there wasn't a seat at the bar, I'd sit underneath the TV and do homework on my phone. Ana and I were both taking classes at the community college, and we had to squeeze in our assignments whenever we could. Every day it was all work, school, work. I had a part-time job at the Little General, but Ana was the one who made the money. She got amazing tips due to how beautiful she was. Guys arrived early to get a seat at the bar so they could be close to her. When she called them by name, they seemed to think they had a special connection. But Ana felt sorry for them. She was studying psychology. She'd listen to their stories, giving them her complete attention like she was their counselor, and then she'd use their stories in class.

Sitting at the bar, they'd tell me how lucky I was. They'd say, "How'd you do it, man?" and I could feel their envy. "What'd you do?"

T.D. punched his key remote, and taillights flashed in the corner of the parking lot: black Civic, no hubcaps. Someone had keyed the whole length of the driver's side, and I wondered what he'd done to make them mad. He got in, I got in. He'd pushed his seat back as far as it would go, and he'd pushed mine back to match it. I had so much leg room, it felt like lounging. I could hardly breathe, the car smelled so bad. It was like sitting in an ashtray, greasy and saturated with smoke. But it was too cold to roll the windows down; they were calling for snow. T.D. started the car, and the heat came on. Stale air blew into my face. He turned and looked at me as if he'd never seen me before. "I take it you don't smoke, right?" he said. "Well then, I won't smoke neither." He reached into his top pocket, pulled out a cigarette, and perched it between his lips without lighting it.

We headed out of town. I wasn't sure where we were going, whether it was his house or someone else's he knew. I asked him to tell me about the cat again. I wanted to get him talking, let him loosen up. It was going to be a long, weird drive. At the bar, he'd always tell Ana, "The kitty's so lonely," and make her pout. He'd add a little whine in his voice to get more sympathy. "The kitty needs somebody to love it, like you," he'd say. You could tell he wanted to feel closer to Ana, like they were going to share the same baby. And if she took the cat, the soft cuddly cat, she'd owe him something.

Now he just shrugged. "It's a fucking cat," he told me, "just a fucking ugly cat. It started coming around my house and wouldn't leave. But I've got to get it off my hands. I'm allergic."

Ana's allergic too, I started to say, but what difference would it make? She was determined. If she started sneezing, she'd just take something. She'd already chosen a name for the cat. Tigger. No matter what the its name was, she was changing it to Tigger. It had to do with a childhood memory in Puerto Rico, the video she and her little sister played over and over.

We turned onto 28 North, and T.D. almost sideswiped an SUV. The driver laid on his horn, and T.D. laid on his, shoving his flat hand on the steering wheel and cutting so hard to the right that we nearly ran up the guardrail. The other driver gunned ahead of us, eyes in his rearview. Through his back windshield we could see him flipping us off. T.D. rolled down his window. "Son of a bitch!" he called, "fucking learn to drive!" Blood rose in his neck, and instantly I saw an older man:

beet-red skin and weary, wrinkled eyes. His cigarette flopped in the corner of his mouth, and he lipped it to keep it from falling. He squeezed the knob of the gear stick. "I could catch that guy in two seconds flat," he said, "but I'll spare you, Rick."

He leaned into the windshield and watched the car disappear up the highway. "Did you see that guy?" he said. "This whole damned country's going to hell. It used to be the blacks, but now it's the Mexicans. They come in by the truckload and work for nothing. They don't even bother to speak English! Just watch what'll happen if we don't stop them—mark my words. After a few years of all those Mexican kids going to school with our kids, everybody will be speaking Spanish. Buenos dias! Might as well start now. I'm surprised that highway sign's not written in Spanish. Twenty-six miles to Green Bank. What's that in Spanish, anyway? What's green in Spanish, what's bank?"

"Banco verde," I said. "Home of the world's largest radio telescope."

"Right-o. That's telescope's one giant motherfucker. Used to be they were discovering clouds on Mercury, but now all they do is listen for aliens. And when they finally do hear the aliens on their super-clear earphones, what do you think they'll hear? Spanish. Those aliens will be speaking Spanish."

He turned on the radio. I said, "You know Ana speaks Spanish." But he didn't hear me. He pulled the unlit cigarette from his dry lips and set it on the dashboard. Then he started singing. It was Tom Petty. We were free-fallin'.

SO HOW DID I do it? Pure luck. I met her on the Fourth of July at a party by the river, the usual keg and fireworks, except this time, she was there. She'd come with somebody I vaguely recognized. They walked up and got beers, and then they stood to the side without talking to anybody. It looked like he was trying to keep her to himself, but who could blame him? She was one of the most beautiful people you ever saw. Caramel skin, long dark hair that curled down her back. And she had this smooth way about her, like she was floating on air. Since the two didn't seem to be hitting it off, I took a chance and introduced myself, and then Ana and I got to talking, and we didn't stop. We talked all night. When the party died down, she left with me, a miracle. A miracle that she liked me that much, a miracle that I was able to get away without getting my ass kicked.

Ana Soto. How this beautiful Puerto Rican girl ended up in Pocahontas County is another miracle. She was born in Fajardo, then her family moved to San Juan. Things happened, and it was just her sister and her mother and her mother's boyfriend, and the three of them moved to the States. To West Virginia—go figure. Puerto Ricans are actually Americans, although nobody seems to know this. I didn't know, either. I drove her back to my house. Fireworks were still going off, so we sat outside listening to them pop. I told her about the telescope. I said, fifty miles from here they're listening for sounds from outer space. We kept drinking. She wanted me to hear her favorite song in Spanish, Chino y Nacho: Me voy enamorando. Me voy, me voy enamorando. She loved me enough to stay.

T.D. TURNED WEST AND began driving toward Cass. He hadn't quit singing. After Tom Petty, it was the Judds, then Styx, then Boston. We'd been listening to a show the girl DJ called "Mixed

Bag of Nuts." T.D. loved it. She was, she kept letting us know, "your little red-headed intern." She'd go, "Howdy everybody, it's your little red-headed intern with a mixed bag of nuts!" Each time she'd say it, T.D. would get this look in his eye. "Yes ma'am, little red-head, you can come sit on my bag of nuts any time." He said it more than once, and I got the feeling he was goading me, like he wanted me to picture him with this red-head sitting on his lap. And the worst part of it was, I did picture it— everything, including the nuts. Horrible. Riding in his Honda, we were sitting so close to each other that our knees touched. He kept rapping the steering wheel, keeping time, and I could see the hairs on the back of his hand. I tried to watch the road, but I kept noticing features I hadn't seen when he was at the bar, like the chicken pox scar on the side of his face, and the way his mouth drooped at the corners.

The sky over the mountains looked bruised. I asked him how much farther we had to go.

"Why," he said, "you getting nervous?" He reached over and turned down the radio.

"What would I be nervous about?" I said.

"I don't know, the sky maybe. The snow."

The red-head began to play a public service announcement, something about suicide prevention. T.D. turned it off. In the quiet, I could detect a wobble in the tires.

I said, "I'd hate to get stuck out here. I told Ana I'd be back before dark. She's looking forward to the cat."

"The cat," T.D. said. He gave me a sideways glance. "The cat needs cleaning up. It's been through a bit of a rough patch. But Ana will take care of it. She'll brush its fur and give it little bowls of milk. I bet she'll even sleep with it under the covers."

Here we went. I knew it'd be just a matter of time.

"What's it like?" he said.

I pretended I didn't know what he was talking about. "What's what like?"

"Ana. I can't even imagine."

"She's good," I said.

"Oh, I'm sure she is, I'm sure she's good."

To say I wanted to punch his face would be accurate. But to say I'd never do this in a million years would also be accurate. All my life, I've made a point of avoiding confrontation. I'm the first one out the door whenever a fight is about to start. At home, in bars, wherever. In bars, you can always tell when a fight's coming on. Chairs scrape the floor, and then there's a lot of shuffling, a knocked-over table or two, and people start stepping back to make room. "Fight!" Inevitably, somebody will shout it to get things rolling. It's then I run.

"Yeah, Ana's good," I said. "A good person. Let's just leave it there."

"No offense, man," he said. "But you gotta admit."

I reached up and rubbed the fog from the windshield. I could hear T.D. sigh. It was a sigh I understood. We were two guys on the highway in the snow, out to get a stupid cat. For Ana, T.D.'s dream. And mine, truth was. She was so much better than me. Beautiful, sexy and kind. What's she like, T.D. wanted to know. Desperately wanted to know. In bed, sure. But what I could've told him, maybe should've told him, was this: she's amazing. She speaks two languages. You feel smarter when you're with her. She's lived far away, she's seen things not everybody sees. She's been out on the ocean. She watched the sun set from the deck of a ship.

She has two words for the moon. Two ways of crying for love. All I had was one.

T.D. took the cigarette from where he'd set it on the dashboard and pushed it between his lips, and then he began flipping it up and down using his tongue. It was a trick, kind of, like when people whistle through a blade of grass or when they flick two fingers to make them snap. This gave me an idea. It was time to change the subject. I said, "Want to see a magic trick?"

He gave me this look, which I got: suddenly I'd turned weird on him. It was like he'd just picked up some freak off the side of the road and let him ride in his car. "Give me a cigarette," I told him. "I won't smoke it—I don't smoke, remember? I'm just going to make it disappear."

Slowly on purpose he took a fresh cigarette from his shirt pocket and handed it to me.

It was one of the first tricks I ever learned. I held the cigarette in front of my hands. "Here you see the cigarette," I said. Then I did this thing that always blows people's minds. With one hand I began tapping the cigarette into the palm of my other hand, tap-tap, and inch by inch it "disappeared." What T.D. couldn't see was how I'd captured the cigarette inside my palm like a little hidden stick. Then I did the wave-the-magic-wand motion with both my hands. I mean, a dove could've flown from my fingers at that point. Out came the cigarette.

"Dang," he said, "you're a regular Houdini. Can you get yourself out of a refrigerator wrapped with chains?"

"I don't remember Houdini escaping from a refrigerator," I said. "Just his Chinese water torture trick. They were all tricks, you know, just illusions. There's an art to it."

"Well here's a story," he said. "When I was growing up, a kid

I knew died in an old refrigerator on his back porch. Climbed in and couldn't get out. He could've used a trick."

We passed a pasture with two horses running along the fence line. They looked like they were trying to keep warm in the cold. The snow had started, flurries mixed with little pellets of ice. "It's getting iffy," I said. T.D. dropped his head as if we were driving under a bridge. He squinted up at the sky. "We're almost there," he said, "I've just got to pick up somebody first."

We found her at the crest of an unpaved driveway that had holes so deep, the Honda scraped the ground like a plow. A woman, maybe forty, standing outside a little brick house in the cold. It was as if she'd known precisely when we'd arrive, although T.D. hadn't phoned her, hadn't even lifted a phone out of his pocket during the whole drive. Out here, there wasn't any service anyway. Her face was buried beneath a scarf, and she had on this long puffy coat. T.D. kept the motor running, and she stepped around to my side. I opened the door so she could get in. The air was freezing; snow was already coating the ground. She stood there looking at me. "So," she said. It was her way of telling me to move. I flipped my seat forward so she could climb in the back. I probably should've gotten out and let her sit in the front, but I didn't think about this at the time. I introduced myself. "I'm Vince."

As soon as I shut the door, she lit up, and we all tasted weed.

She'd planted herself so perfectly behind me that I couldn't see her at all, not even the edge of her coat. With T.D. at my side, and with her eyeing me from behind, I felt trapped. Once the two began talking to each other, it was more like I'd been kidnapped. She smoked her joint with noisy enthusiasm, squeezing in every inhale. It was sort of hard to listen to. After a few minutes, she said, "Any word from Lyman?" T.D. glanced back at her. "Nah." She took a last toke and settled back, kneeing my seat, and then she said, "I don't blame him for running. Don't blame him at all." T.D. turned on the radio, but the little red-head's show had ended, so he turned it off.

We were pushing on through light snow. In the distance, the mountains were totally hidden behind thick clouds. I considered asking T.D. for a pit stop, but then I thought better of it. I wanted us to keep going. Plus, I didn't relish the idea of standing behind the bumper taking a leak with her along. I ventured a question. "So what about that cat?"

"What cat?" she said. She leaned over my shoulder, her face close to mine. She smelled like weed smoke and something sweet, like she'd just finished a glass of milk.

"You know, the cat," T.D. said. "The one we gotta get rid of."

"Is that why he's here?" she said. "Is that what's up?"

"Yep," he said. "I'm doing him a favor. He's got a girl, and she's in love with cats."

"A kitty-cat girl," she said. There was a hint of nastiness in her voice, like the only people who love cats are crazy people. Like, a cat's nothing more than a mouse catcher. A cat's what you drown.

FARTHER UP THE HIGHWAY, we turned and started off-road, driving over fresh snow into the forest. It was the kind of snow that sticks to everything. Tree limbs sagged in our path, slushing across the windshield. On a steep incline, T.D. downshifted, and our rear tires began to spin. We were fishtailing through trees.

He white-knuckled the steering wheel, and then suddenly we were cruising along an invisible driveway, and there was a clearing up ahead, our apparent destination. Two little houses, some sheds, and a fleet of cars and trucks, some clearly not drivable. So here was where the cat was.

The scene took me back to my great-uncle's place outside Harrisonburg. Uncle Bob Knott, world-class hoarder of engines. He liked to sleep outside in his car, but there were so many cars on his property that it was hard to find him.

T.D. got out and headed toward the better of the two houses, the one with the screened porch and the flag. He hiked up his jeans. From the back seat, I heard, "Aren't you going to let me out?" I lifted the door handle. "Yeah," I said, "but first you need to tell me your name." I stepped out and held the door. During the drive, her scarf had settled around her neck, exposing her face. It was a shock, her face. Red-rimmed eyes and skin so lemon-colored that it looked like she'd been in a wreck. She gripped the inside of the doorframe so as to pull herself out, and I saw how selfish I was to have kept the front seat to myself. "I'm Margaret Dinkens," she said, "T.D.'s sister. And his name's Ted, by the way. Over in that other house is our father. And wandering somewhere in the Dolly Sods right now is our baby brother, who's about to freeze to death in the cold."

The house she'd pointed to was so small and closed-up, it looked like nobody lived there. But that's where her father was, apparently. Or rather, their father—hers and the runaway's and T.D.'s. Or should I say, Ted's. Knowing his real name left me feeling kind of gut-punched. I pictured a little boy. How proud you've made us, Ted.

She started toward the house, but I took my time. I didn't look forward to joining the family. She stepped on the porch, knocked the snow off her shoes, and slipped inside, leaving me in the cold.

I stood listening to snow falling through the trees. There was sleet mixed in, so it made a nice sizzling sound. Everything was gray. Gray sky, gray houses, gray sheds, and an empty pen with one of those gray plastic doghouses shaped like an igloo. No sign of a dog, only a snow-coated chain. A little ways off, I could detect something hanging from a tree limb. I walked closer and saw a doe, nose down, inches from the ground. Her two hind legs had been bound with rope, her belly slit by a knife. A fresh kill. Someone had been hunting. Somehow I didn't think it was T.D.

The door to the house opened, and he walked out on the porch. He set down a trash bag, then went back inside. I was pissed that I was being ignored. All I wanted was to see him come out with the cat in his arms and say let's go. Because it was getting late. Daylight was fading before my eyes.

The door opened again, and it was Margaret this time. She had a toddler latched to her hip, hanging on like a monkey. I let out a little whistle and Margaret startled, as if she'd forgotten I was out there. "Oh, you!" she said. "Hold on a minute, we've got to go see about Daddy." T.D. stepped out and followed her. They went around to the back of the little closed-up house. I tried trailing them, but T.D. stopped me. He took a long, serious drag from his cigarette. "Sorry, Rick," he said, "but we've got things we need to tend to. Go next door and make yourself at home."

I could feel the afternoon turning strange; it was like they were playing a game of cups and balls. Without seeing the daddy hidden inside, I could only picture the invalid he might be. There was a shitty ramp behind his house, and all his windows had been covered with plastic. I began taking inventory. Later, Ana would appreciate the details. Beginning with the deer, its fur blanketed in snow, and then the wench and the cable clamped to a far tree, and the rusting Volvo on blocks, and the rusted old refrigerator and the propane tank nestled in its cradle like a giant white pill.

All for you, Ana.

I DECIDED TO MAKE myself at home. But when I crossed the porch and pushed open the door, I found a girl. She was sitting on the couch with her shirt unbuttoned, eyes closed. She looked like she might be meditating, or maybe she was just settling in on a good high. The room was a sauna. I looked for the cause and found a space heater, coils neon bright. I didn't know what to do: I had to use the john, but I didn't want to disturb the girl. So I eased away, keeping an eye on her in case she came to. She was probably the toddler's mother, still breast-feeding. Also probably, she belonged to Lyman, the baby brother now wandering in the Dolly Sods. I inched down the hallway past a bedroom and peeked in. There was stuff all over the floor, clothes and shoes and what-not, but the bed was made, and there was a prom picture hanging over the headboard. I kept on down the hall toward the bathroom. I could've found it with my eyes closed, it smelled so bad. But it wasn't the toilet, lid up, unflushed, and it wasn't the sour wash rag balled in the sink, it was the cat. Bone-thin, ripped fur, draining eyes. They were keeping the cat in an animal trap they'd set down in the tub. So they could wash away the mess it made.

The cat began rubbing its back against the wire, back and forth, back and forth, peeling off tufts of white fur. This would be Tigger. A sick, vomitous cat. I took a leak and fled. Or, should I say, I left the cat behind and crept back up the hall to where the girl was. By then she'd dropped her head against the back of the couch and started to snore. You could see the tendons in her neck and the bones of her throat. Skinny, like the cat.

Something in the kitchen caught my eye. It was one of those kitchens that's open to the den, with bar stools. A flash of movement on a small monitor propped on the counter: a home video. It was T.D., and he was lugging something across a floor. Somewhere in the other house, there was a camera. Recording everything. On the screen, Margaret ran in and out. She was waving her arms as if giving directions. Now it was T.D. waving: stand back. They were dragging their dad across the room, I could see his bony, cadaverous face turning side to side. He wasn't dead, though, just immobile. And from what I could tell by viewing a notebook-sized screen on mute, he was screaming. I stood in front of the monitor as if watching a horror show. T.D. positioned himself behind his father with a hand beneath each underarm and lifted him into a wheelchair while Margaret held the chair steady. They got him all in. And then, to my unbelieving eyes, the old man wheeled himself out of view.

A minute passed, and T.D. and Margaret appeared on the monitor again. Margaret had the toddler in her arms, and she was headed toward the door. They were going to leave the old man behind in his house, most likely because it's hard to wheel a chair through snow, and they were coming back over to get me. I sat on one of the bar stools pretending to mind my own business. On one side of me, I had a sleeping mama on a couch, and on the other side I had a hubcap full of cigarette butts. I heard T.D. and Margaret stomp across the porch and push open the door. I was ready. I said, "Everything all right?" I acted like I hadn't seen them on the monitor, like I hadn't even noticed there was a monitor at all, the screen on the counter with a view of a now-empty room.

T.D. said, "So did you see my dad on the screen over there?" I shrugged, maybe. "Sometimes he gets out of his chair, and we have to help him up. But I'll tell you one thing, he's a damned good shot. He might be paralyzed, but he can still hunt."

The girl came to, purple-eyed and confused. She glanced in my direction and gave me a blank, stunned look, and then she reached for the toddler. Margaret set him down on the girl's lap, and she pulled him close. "So who's this guy?" she said.

"This is Rick," T.D. said. "He's come to get the cat."

"Vince," I said.

The girl started picking at the toddler's face, but the kid didn't utter a sound. She reached over to pull a cigarette from the pack on the table. One-handed, she put the cigarette in her lips, took up a Bic, and lit up. She drew in a long inhale and blew smoke across the toddler's head. And then she stopped still, as if she was considering something serious. "The cat?" she said, "he's come to get that cat? How about the baby? He can have a baby and a cat." She ran a hand across the toddler's light hair. "Two for one, Bo-Bo."

"She's just kidding," T.D. said.

"Every baby needs a father, and every mother needs a husband. That's what I'm saying."

"That's enough, Trish," Margaret said. "Cool it."

"I'm just saying what's obvious. If this good-looking guy here needs a cat, I say give him what he needs, double-time. A cat and his very own sex slave, there's a bargain for you. I could make him so happy, he'd never run off."

T.D. wheeled on one foot as if he might punch something, and Margaret raised her voice. "I said, enough."

"A guy cute as him."

I saw something flash across the monitor screen. The dad was wheeling through his house. I didn't think he could hear us, but you never know.

The toddler began to paw at his mother's neck. She lowered a bra strap and pushed forth one of her breasts. He nestled in, and she looked up at me. "You know, he's a sweet one," she said.

T.D. had had enough. "I'm thinking it's time to go," he said, "before things turn crazy." He went down the hall and came back with the animal trap lifted over his head, the cat struggling to stay on its feet.

"Here comes stinky!" Trish said.

T.D. lowered the trap to the floor and stared down at it. "This thing's too big to fit in the car, so we'll have to pull out the cat and let it ride on the seat."

The cat was so scared, it drooled.

"Is that what you really want?" Trish said, accusing me. "That?"

Margaret chimed in. "Poor thing," she said, "it doesn't have a brain. Each time we throw it out, it comes back."

I got down on my knees to get a better look at the cat, and all eyes turned on me. "So how do I open this trap?"

T.D. stood above me and lifted the trap door, but the cat didn't budge. I leaned in and whispered, "It's okay."

"Watch your face!" Trish said. "Get ready, it's gonna bolt!"

The cat lunged, and I caught it by the neck.

"Nice work," Trish said.

I squeezed the cat's neck and gripped its hind legs. I've had a good number of cats in my life.

"Let's go before it gets dark," T.D. said.

He'd found a red knit beanie on top of the toaster oven and slipped it over his head. I followed him out, the cat squirming in my arms. I gripped it tight, and it released a stink.

TO SAY I'D DO anything for Ana Soto was true. It's my pleasure, Ana, I liked to say, I'll do anything you want. Anything to satisfy you, to make your life easier, to make you happy. I knew what a risk this was; I didn't want to overdo it. But she was so self-assured and beautiful that it was like she'd come from a place where everybody was born cool. Not to mention that you couldn't stop looking at her face: her bright white teeth, her smooth brown skin, her delicate mouth. Someday I knew I'd probably have to fight for her, and to this, she'd say: Don't be ridiculous.

Oh, but it was true.

When T.D. and I got to the car, he cleared the snow from the windshield, hacked away the ice on his door handle, and slid in. He started the motor and looked up at me through the foggy window: get in. But I was fighting with the cat. It clawed across my chest as if I was a tree, snagging holes in my jacket, and I squeezed it so tight, I could feel its ribs bend. I looked down at the car door. I'd have to break the ice on the handle, open it, and get in without losing the cat. It was a trick, but I managed it. With one hand, I shattered the ice and opened the door. Then I fell into the seat with the cat. T.D. pushed the car into gear, and we were off. Second gear, then third. I looked out into the darkening sky and said a prayer to the gods. That the snow wouldn't fall any harder than it was already. That we wouldn't get stuck in a blizzard, me and T.D. Plus this stinking cat.

We spun out the same way we'd spun in, dodging trees. Snow-coated pines arched across our path. We kept ducking our heads as if to save ourselves. I turned the cat loose. It sprang to the back and began rubbing the seat, crying. It sounded like a cat in heat, and then it occurred to me: it was.

The Honda dragged through snow. You could feel the ground beneath the floorboards. I had to shout above the noise. "What do you know about the cat?"

"Nothing," T.D. shouted back. "Nada. It's just a piece of shit."

He lit a cigarette and blew smoke into the windshield. "But Ana will love it. Love it to death."

I set my eyes on the headbeams as if I was the one in control. "Watch up ahead, that tree. Here's another one, watch it." It felt like we were the only living things in the forest, the only ones left in the whole world, just us. Except for the cat, which was now so wired and noisy that I wanted to toss it out the window.

We reached the highway. The last quarter-mile before we got there, the Honda had been so low to the ground that it looked like we might stall out. But we made it, and the ride improved. The highway hadn't been plowed yet, but there'd been enough traffic to clear a visible path. It got quiet. For a while, even the cat settled down.

We were en route to Cass, and then we'd turn south toward home. Ana would be at work by then, which meant I'd have to take care of the cat by myself. I started thinking about what to feed it and whether it was possible to give it a bath. Nobody gives a cat a bath, but this one smelled so bad, we'd have to try it, maybe put on long sleeves and gloves, oven mitts, to keep from getting scratched to hell. Then I remembered: the cat was in heat. What do you do with a cat in heat?

T.D. lit another cigarette. He leaned over the steering wheel with his cigarette in one hand, pointing it upward, watching the smoke rise.

I did the wrong thing. Looking back, I can see it. I said: "So where's Lyman?"

He dropped back in his seat and turned his face to me. He clenched his teeth; it was like he had a seed in there. "Now that's a story I'm not willing to tell."

"He ran away?"

He spit out the invisible seed, rolled down his window and tossed the cigarette. Then he began to massage the steering wheel, really work it, kneading it hard. "Like I said, Rick."

I turned on the radio to the sound of static, and the cat sprang from the back and perched on my shoulder, claws out. She clung close to my ear, wheezing like an asthmatic, back legs ready to leap to the dashboard. I gripped her with one hand and held her back, and she smelled so pukey, I had to catch my breath.

"Jesus," T.D. said. "That cat's gotta go."

I sat perfectly still in so as to calm the cat, and it crawled into my lap. I said, "Let's just listen to music. You know a good radio station out here?"

"How about we keep it quiet instead?" he said. "How about we just hold it down."

He tugged his knit cap over his forehead until all you could see was just a big, smooth skull, bright red, with brows.

As if the cat was thinking the same thing I was, that T.D.

looked like something alien, she climbed onto his headrest and swatted his head, snagging a single claw in the knit of his cap. He threw an elbow and sent her flying. She let out a screechy cry and flopped across the back seat, a dull slap. We began to skid. "Steady," I said. T.D. steered into the skid, and the car straightened. Incredibly, he took this opportunity to accelerate. Sixty miles per hour, in snow. I braced myself.

"What do you say we kill it?" he said.

"What?" I said.

"The cat. What'd you think I meant, what else might we kill? Fill me in on that, Bud. You see this cap on my head? Did you ever think, when you buy something new to wear, that you might just die in it? That the thing you like turns out to be the thing you die in? Not saying I'm going die in this cap, but everybody's gotta die in something."

We raced across the gray landscape. T.D. kept talking. "Let's just say Lyman couldn't take it anymore, let's just say things got so fucked up, he didn't have a choice, he had to get the hell out. Which is all fine and good for him, but then guess what? Somebody's gotta pick up the pieces. And guess who that is."

"I'm sorry," I said.

He lit another cigarette, hands shaking. "I don't need your sympathy."

We had about twenty minutes of daylight left. I could see the snow beginning to taper off. We'd gotten maybe four inches, total. I thought about Ana, which made me think about the cat. I wanted to turn around to see if it was still alive, but I didn't dare: I needed to concentrate on the road. We were still speeding. If we spun out, I wanted to be ready. I listened for the sound of the cat's wheezing breath, but it was so quiet back there, I thought

T.D. might've actually killed it after all, which could be for the best. No telling what the cat had been through in its life. Some stranger probably dropped it off on the road, and it followed its nose to the closest warm thing. Which would've been its most unlucky move.

But the cat did make noise again, a thin, creaky sound. "There she blows," T.D. said. He opened the glove box and pulled out a gun. He gave me a sly look. "Where should I put this?"

In his heavy hand, the gun wobbled before my eyes, a flat, nickel-finish pistol like nothing I'd ever seen before, antique.

I tried to be cool. I said, "How about between us, right here," and he laid the gun on top of the handbrake.

"So that's not for the cat, is it?" I said.

"Nope, not unless you say so."

I could hear her wheezing back there, and I could tell she'd started rubbing the seat again. I looked out the side window to keep from looking down at the gun. There was a sliver of pink light over the mountains, and it looked so hopeful, I almost choked up.

"It wouldn't hurt me a bit to toss that cat out in the snow," T.D. said. "And I'd do if you'd let me. You could just tell Ana it escaped."

"She really wants it," I said.

"Yeah, I know she does. That's my girl Ana, she loves her animals. She's told me all about how she grew up in Puerto Rico with lots of pets. She once had a little goat."

"She never had a goat," I said. "She lived in San Juan, it's a city."

"Well, that's what they like to call it. But it's still primitive as hell. It's a good thing Ana was able to get out of there."

"Yeah, a really good thing for me, I'd say." I knew I shouldn't have said it, but I couldn't resist.

Still, he didn't seem to hear me. He said, "I know a lot about Ana that you don't know, Rick."

"It's Vince."

"Whatever," he said. "Ana just might be the most beautiful woman I've ever laid my eyes on. I tell you what, I hope you don't mind me saying this, but I'd like to have just one taste of her. Just one taste."

He lifted his foot off the accelerator and the car started to slow. He smiled to himself. "Just one little teensy taste between her thighs."

I felt my heart race, hot blood rushing in my ears. "Shit," I said, "Come on."

"Sorry, man, it's true. She must be one amazing fuck."

I suddenly felt so bad for Ana that I felt heat behind my eyes. It was a weird reaction I didn't expect. T.D. didn't know the first thing about her; she was nothing to him. I looked down at the gun. It was compact, about the same size as a pack of cards.

"So," he went on, "what'd you do to get her? How'd you manage it, Rick, a little guy like you. A little pussy like you."

I reached for the gun, but he got there first. "Thought you'd get tricky," he said. He held the gun barrel-up, finger on the trigger, and pulled to the side of the road. We were in the middle of nowhere. The last sign I saw was for Dunmore. Before that, it was Green Bank, going in the other direction. Out where the telescope was, where the physics majors were listening to the stars.

"What'd you plan to do with the gun if you got it, huh?" T.D. said. "How far were you willing to go? Did you think you'd shoot me? Really?"

"I'll get out right here," I said. "No problem, it's cool." I opened my door, and in a flash, the cat leapt out and disappeared. White cat, white snow, gone—a ghost. "I can walk," I said.

T.D. held the gun in his hand, not pointing it anywhere. I got out, slowly. I didn't want to turn my back. I stepped off a few feet and gave him a look that said, I surrender. He paused and looked me square in the face, a solemn, dull look in his eyes, and lifted the gun. But instead of pointing it at me, he turned it on himself, square at his temple. I held my breath. I didn't know what to do. It was a long wait. And then he lowered the gun and pulled away, slowly, leaving me behind in the dark. I watched his red tail lights go.

I was stranded, but I was alive. I started walking, keeping close to the edge of the highway in case a truck came along. Judging by the lack of stars, the sky was still cloudy, which was a good thing. There's nothing colder than a clear night winter sky—that's what I thought, or that's what I think now. It could've been worse, I could've frozen. I walked, my head filled with the image of a gun to a temple and saw how close we'd both been to the brink.

BIRTHDAY II

The end of summer and the boys are all out on the deck around the piñata. It's a solid mass of newspaper and wheat paste, heavy as a sack of wet grass. A homemade piñata, okay? So I made it myself to save money.

The boys are trying to figure out what it's supposed to be. I won't tell them dog, although that's what it looks like, because no kid should think it's a game to beat a dog with a big stick. One of them says it, says, "It's a dog!" But I shake my head even though he's right, it pretty much looks like a dog. Then another one guesses it's a cat, and I say no again, although it wouldn't hurt me much if they started swinging at a cat.

So now they shout guesses. "A horse! A cow! A moose!" I shake my head no to each one—I want them to think, to use their imagination, you know. They stand there a second, looking, and then a kid shouts, "It's a dog," which you could predict. There's a kid like that in every bunch, one who's missing a connection in his brain, not paying a bit of attention to anything that's going on. Finally I announce that it's a mule, which stuns them. I only thought of it two seconds ago. Not one of them even knows what a mule *is*. Fine, I say, let me tell you: it's a cross between a donkey and a horse—so line up.

I tie a blindfold over the eyes of the first one, twirl him around to disorient him, and hand him the stick. It's an old broom handle. He holds it in both hands as if he means to kill somebody, then starts swinging like a drunk, he's so dizzy. "Whoa there," I tell him, "take it easy, bud," and pull off the blindfold. "You could kill somebody." Then one by one, it's the same routine: blindfold, twirl, stick, swipe. I know I should leave out the "twirl" part, but it's such a kick to see them stagger around that I twirl them all. The boys love it but they hate it, too. They want to get a good hit in, but they can't tell which way is up, so they swing wildly, nearly lopping off each other's heads, each aiming to crack the mule in half.

After about ten minutes of this they start getting frustrated. The mule hangs dumbly, poster-painted red and blue, which are the only colors I had. "Stupid mule!" one of them shouts. "Yeah! Stupid ugly MULE!" So I let the next kid peek. I tie the blindfold loose, twirl him just a little, then let him go *thwack!* a solid hit, but the mule's barely dented. The next kid, same thing, only a bigger dent. The next, a little hole in the side.

It's about this time I look at my watch. The birthday party's almost over, the mothers will start showing up soon. I've got to move this thing along, got to get this party on the road, so I take the broom handle in my hand, say, "My turn!" and give it to the mule, really give it to him until it spins and lands on the deck with a thud. The boys rush in and start kicking at it, but it's like kicking wet paper so they start stomping, and next thing I know I'm in the middle, stomping too, until I realize it's not a paper mule I'm stomping, it's Cathy, and I'm thinking how if she was still here we'd have a decent piñata and a real cake with Mikie's name on it and nobody would be crying like they are right now, and the candy, oh crap the candy, the one thing I forgot when I made the damned piñata, the candy.

THE BLAMING HEART

*I really believe life is simple. It's all the
other people that make things complicated.*

—RICHARD NIXON

Roz Nicolaides walked through the bright comfort of the liquor store, Scotch-Bourbon-Cognac-Gin. Arriving at gin, a fifth of Beefeater. Because a little gin never killed anybody. Next she'd pick up some tonic at the grocery store. And what else would she pick up? Because Elaine and Matt were coming to town, a rump roast. Also eggs, bacon, and cereal, breakfast things for Matt. He of the woolly head and chainsaw.

Matt was Elaine's choice. Or rather, God's choice, since Elaine began praying for her husband when she was baby. "Somewhere, right now, he's out there, mama," she said once while riding in the car. She was fourteen years old. "He might be riding in a car with his mom too, just like me. He might be practicing the piano or playing baseball."

Matthew Duckworth, a stocky kid who never did play baseball. It was hard to imagine him even breaking into a run. Instead he was a sculptor. He could do wonders with a tree trunk, a chain saw, and a chisel. Already he'd sold three of his creations. One, a giant bust of a pilgrim, he'd sold for two hundred dollars to Pilgrim Pride Auto. Elaine called it an answered prayer. Matt claimed he'd just tapped into a universal idea.

Everybody's a pilgrim.

In Raleigh he'd worked on the McGovern campaign, confessed it was the first thing he ever believed in. Roz was sure it was because of George McGovern that Matt started smoking pot. All over the country kids smoked pot at McGovern headquarters, did they not? Amazing, that these young people, stoned out of their minds, thought McGovern would actually win the election! Even more amazing was that Elaine, of her three children the most innocent, the most devout, joined the McGovern crowd. At their victory-turned-defeat party. At news of McGovern's defeat, Matt apparently burst into tears, and apparently Elaine comforted him.

The mystery of it all. That Elaine would end up at the McGovern party. That she would not only be introduced to Matt Duckworth, but that she would "comfort him." Comfort an anarchist. Or if not an anarchist, a smart mouth who liked to argue too much. Or debate. He liked to debate too much. Would he cut his hair in order to get a job? No, he would not. Because would a woman be expected to cut her hair for a job? No, so why a man? And did the government have the right to tell you what you can and cannot do on your own property? Let's say you bought a peacock—as long as it didn't scream all the time, what difference would it make to the government, or to your neighbors, for that matter? Live and let live.

Roz stopped at a light, and the bottle of gin rolled off the seat.

Fortunately it didn't break, because thinking about Matt made her want to have a drink. When Matt and Elaine came through the door later, a little drink would help. She'd been warned by Nick already: do not argue with that kid. Last time he came for a visit, they'd all been having a nice dinner, with Nick at the head of the table and she at the other end, everybody behaving, when Matt started going on about Watergate. Just you wait, he declared, this whole thing's going to blow up, it's a ticking time bomb! When nobody had much to say about Watergate, he started in on the subject of art. His art. He bragged that his sculpted trunks of trees sprang from an imagination freed from tradition. He was, as a matter of fact, considering going to art school. Or maybe joining a sculpture colony down in Arkansas. They let you work in the wild, he said, where you can go large.

He looked at Roz. "Precisely the opposite of your art," he said. "Whereas my work is free and muscular, yours is a settled, prescribed, feminine craft."

This stung. Scherenschnitte, the Dutch tradition of paper cutting, was her love. Roz's cheeks burned, and she fumbled for words. "Scherenschnitte," Matt said finally, "while beautiful, doesn't qualify as art at all. It's like lace. And nobody would refer to lace as art."

She'd sat at dinner feeling the weight of scissors in her hand. How dare he look down on her art. She was tempted to jump up from the table and take a snip out of his hair. She could have told him, if she'd not been so humiliated and filled with rage, that the holes in paper represented negative space. She might have impressed him with that. Instead she attacked his sculpture. Anybody can cut a piece of wood with a chain saw, she'd said, it doesn't take talent! Chop, chop—what sort of skill did that take? As for chiseling, that wasn't much harder. If you chiseled off a piece you hadn't meant to chisel, what you got was a lucky mistake. If you started out making a sculpture of an eagle and accidentally chopped off a wing, then you could just chop off the other wing and make a beaver!

Later, Elaine insisted that she apologize. "I just might marry him, Mama," she said.

AT HOME IN THE Nicolaides yard, an orange tabby lay in the sun. Punky. When Elaine's sister Ann stepped outside holding a phone, its long cord dragging behind her, he didn't budge. Ann looked at the cat without really looking at him. Here she was, home against her will, grounded for lying. It was all because of a street party last Saturday. About fifty kids were there, cars lined up along the curb. And then cops came. She wasn't arrested, but her license plate number was taken down. One thing led to another, and her parents found out. She'd told them she was going to a movie. Instead she was running wild in Brookwood, a new development under construction, just pavement and street-lights and moths. And a whole lot of people.

"We don't care whether there were two people out there or a hundred," her father had said. "What matters is that you lied."

What they didn't know was, the balcony they'd added to the back of their old house made a perfect platform for sneaking out. After midnight, once everybody was asleep, Ann would tiptoe out on the balcony with two bed sheets tied together, loop them over the balcony rail, and slide to the ground. It was a trick she'd seen on TV.

She could have easily tiptoed downstairs and slipped out the back door, but that would wake up Punky, and he'd start wandering around the house yowling the way old cats do. It had happened once, and she'd spent the next morning trying to explain why she'd gone outside in the middle of the night. She blamed it on an owl. She'd heard an owl hooting, so she went outside to hear it better. For extra credit in Field Bio. Her father was skeptical. "So what kind of owl was it?" It was a little test. "Horned," she told him.

She loved sneaking out; she was addicted to it. Sneaking out was better than just walking out the door—there was danger involved. Such as that time she sneaked out and waited in the dark at the end of the driveway, and then headlights appeared, and she dropped back waiting to see if it might be who she thought it was—and it was, it was Brian Enzinger—and he slowed down and pulled over to pick her up. In the glow of the dashboard he looked amazing. She got in, and he switched off the headlights. There was a moment of hesitation—he was building suspense—and then he gunned the engine, zero to fifty in about two seconds. When he switched the headlights back on, they were feet away from a parked car. Crazy. He'd been tripping all day. Or the time she met up with friends and they went to Brookwood to drink Roma Rocket and accidentally set the woods on fire. First it was just a few smoking saplings, but then one burst into flames, it was like when you burn a Christmas tree, so they jumped up and ran before the fire trucks came. No one ever knew whom to blame.

"Elaine's coming home from college," she said into the phone. "She's bringing her boyfriend."

She watched her mother drive up the driveway. Punky rose from his nap and walked across the grass toward the car. "I gotta go," she said, "my mom's home." The car door opened, and the cat jumped in.

IN THE KITCHEN, ROZ began going over the plans for the evening. Since Matt was coming to visit, the girls would have to share Ann's room while Matt took Elaine's.

"I don't see why Matt can't stay in Gus's room," Ann said.

Gus's room: a single bed and headboard shaped like a wagon wheel, a cluttered study desk, lighted aquariums, a poster of Mark Spitz. Gus hardly ever came out of there. "It's awful small," Roz said, "Where would Matt sleep?"

"On the floor. What do you think guys do when they stay over at each other's house? Sleep in beds? Besides, Elaine will probably sneak into her room to sleep with Matt anyway."

Roz set a bag of groceries on the counter and tried not to imagine Elaine lying in bed with Matt. She looked over at Ann, who'd picked up a new issue of *Cosmopolitan*. This was what the world had come to.

"Let's not sit around reading that trash. Try to make yourself useful. Go up to your room and make space for Elaine. Pick your stuff off the floor. Then you can come down and feed the cat."

After Ann left the room, Roz took a look at the magazine's cover story: *The Living Together Handbook—Everything You Need to Know (Works Perfectly for Married Couples Too)*. Boy, would she love to see that handbook. Say her mother wrote it, her first rule would be: To live together in peace, let your man be the man. What the magazine probably said: Be classy in public and sexy at home. Her mother: Cook delicious meals he loves and don't be bossy. The magazine: Run your fingers across the back of his neck.

It was only four-thirty, but Roz fixed a drink anyway. She lit a cigarette. Why did she have to go and think about her mother now? She'd been dead ten years, yet there she was, her judge and jury. After the War, when everybody started talking about doing new things, moving to the city, going to college, starting a business, Roz declared that she was going to buy a bus ticket to New York and enroll in the Barbizon School. She had a life to live. But no. No, no, no. Everybody told her she had the perfect figure to be a model, but in the eyes of her mother, the singular, staid Margie Grass, being a model was tantamount to being a streetwalker, so she had to settle for shorthand classes in Asheville. Which led her to meet Nick, the new pharmacist at the Rexall. Dark brown hair, dark eyes, handsome in his white druggist's jacket. Roz fell in love. Her mother, though, blew up. Here she'd raised Roz alone, Roz's daddy having been deceased at the age of twenty-five, and Roz had fallen in love with a foreigner. They married anyway, marching around the altar in a Greek Orthodox Church wearing rings on their heads.

Roz pulled a stool to the kitchen counter and looked out the window to the back yard. Spring had arrived—bees in the grass, Easter baskets and colored eggs, bunnies. They'd given the kids baby chicks one year, real baby chicks that were so cute you wanted to squeeze them. Ann wasn't even four years old yet. She hugged her little chicken hard against her chest. It was all Roz and Nick could do to keep her from smothering it. The chicks died anyway, one by one. Cats got two of them. The other just died. Those were the days. Three children, all under the age of six. Cats, baby chickens, tadpoles—they'd done all the things you do when you're raising kids, like heating up a can of Spaghetti-O's and filling up the sandbox and blowing bubbles in the yard.

Now all that remained was the old swing set, a paint-chipped frame of steel with two chains hanging from the crossbar.

Roz put her lips to her glass and let them stay there, taking in the fragrance of gin. There was something in one of the trees, high in the branches. She leaned close to the window to get a better look. A hornet nest. Funny she hadn't seen it before. Who knew how long it had been there, and all that time she'd mowed the grass, and she and Nick had sat out there in lawn chairs, and Ann and her friends had slipped out there at night, probably to smoke, and no one had known. Hornets were making a nest as big as a football, and they never noticed. Nick was allergic— what if he'd been stung? It had happened once when he was a boy, and he nearly died. What if they'd been sitting out in the yard one evening and he'd gotten up from his chair to toss a stick over the fence and hornets had swarmed down and stung him? He would've gone into shock and they would've called an ambulance and then who knows.

She must warn him.

Punky walked into the kitchen and jumped on Roz's lap. She spoke to him as if he were a person. It was something she did when she was alone—talk to the cat. Nick once said when they began dating that if she didn't change, she'd wind up being an old maid with a house full of cats. It was his way of telling her to let down her guard and give in to him. Well, so she did.

THEY ROLLED IN AT five, Matt behind the wheel of Elaine's car. Ann looked out the window and watched them drive up. "Here they are," she said, "and they've boxed me in." The kitchen smelled of roasting meat and fried onions. Roz opened the oven door to check the roast and thought about Matt driving Elaine's Toyota, a gift they'd given her when she went away to college. It belonged to Elaine, not Matt. "We'll have to speak to Elaine about that," she said. "And it's not you they've boxed in, it's me. Go out and tell her she'll have to move her car."

Ann went out the door and Roz followed. She wanted to catch Matt behind the wheel of Elaine's car and say something to him, remind him that it wasn't his car, but she was too late—they were already out in the yard. Matt had a beard now, and his fuzzy hair curled at his neck the way it did the last time she saw him, only now his cheeks had become blemished with acne. She took in the rest of him: slouchy jeans, scuffed square-toed boots, a ring of keys dangling from his belt.

There proceeded the ritual of hugging. She hugged Matt —an obligatory in-and-out hug that allowed her to catch his odor, which was oddly sweet—and then she hugged Elaine. "You'll have to move the car," she said in her ear. She gave Matt a side-ways glance. "I guess you didn't know where to park, but you've boxed me in."

The girls walked into the house, chattering. Why, Ann wanted to know, was Matt driving her car now? Didn't that feel sort of weird?

"Why not let him drive?" Elaine said. "I kind of like it when he drives."

"But it makes you look married."

"Well what's wrong with that? Anyway, we might actually get married soon."

Roz felt her face flush. "Oh no, you won't," she said.

Elaine looked ready to talk back, but Ann pulled her aside. "Just ignore her," she whispered. "It's not worth it. I think she's going through the change."

The girls disappeared upstairs, and then Matt came in, followed by Gus. They walked through the kitchen and out of sight, leaving Roz alone. The room grew quiet, and she felt a pang of emptiness. How was it that she, a grown woman, now felt ignored? This was absurd—she didn't need them as friends! And she was not going through "the change," she wanted them to know. Even if she was, it was none of their business. What if she went around the house talking about Ann's cramps? Or what if she announced that Nick was having male problems? What would the girls say to that?

They were upstairs laughing now. It was as if they were having a slumber party up there. Nick would enjoy this, if only he were home, if only he could pull himself away from that back pharmacy before nine o'clock every night. People even called him "doctor." Well, every man had to be king of some kind of castle. Nick sat in his swivel chair all day counting out pills and pasting labels on bottles, canned music playing throughout the store, while back at home in her own excuse for a castle Roz made sure the beds were made and the refrigerator was full and the meals were prepared and the cat was fed and the kids were safe and out of trouble, if that was even possible anymore. Not to mention the house. Keeping up with the house was also her job—the constant cleaning and straightening up, the laundry and dishes and bathtubs and floors, the cleaning of baseboards and drapes, the cat hair and cat bowl. "I am a turtle and this house is my shell," she once said to Nick. "I may as well strap this house on my back and carry it around all day." He laughed.

He didn't get it. There had to be more to marriage is what she meant. And there had been, once, but things had a way of dwindling down.

No wonder she'd taken to cutting paper. She'd read about it in the library newsletter listing art classes—decoupage, macramé, Scherenschnitte. In this way she could learn something new, folding paper one sheet at a time and cutting out traditional motifs. The spreading branches of a tree (all those intricate cuts between each tiny branch and leaf), the figures of children following the Pied Piper across a meadow (the Piper's slender flute, the shoots of grass waving in air), and the nearly impossible Noah's Ark.

Everybody had to be the king of something. Or queen. Everybody had to have "their thing."

Once, when she and Nick were first married and they hadn't had kids yet, they went on a vacation in the Smokies. It was their own little getaway, a venture into the wild. For five dollars a night they slept in a Lake Lure cabin that was so old it was as if Daniel Boone built it, and every night they lit a lantern and made love on a dank mattress laid on a frame made of rope. In the morning when light filled the cabin and they opened their eyes, their bodies stiff and cold and sore, Nick would look at Roz and call her his queen. It was all because of a dream he'd had, an absurd dream about horses and knights and Roz wearing a crown. When he awoke, he turned on the mattress and gazed at Roz lying next to him and said, still dreaming, "Roz, honey, what are you queen of?"

She looked up at the planks of the ceiling and blinked. In the dawn light the cabin was hazy and dark. Queen?

"Queen," he whispered.

"Queen," she repeated. "Queen bee."

She went outside to retrieve the evening paper. She unrolled it and looked at the headlines. Nixon was fixing beef prices. The last POWs had been released from Vietnam.

BY THE TIME THEY sat down to dinner, Roz had had too much gin. She knew she shouldn't have done it, but she had. Ann had set the table in such a spirit of resentment that Roz wished she hadn't bothered. They'd argued. Roz kept reminding Ann to lower her voice—"we have company"—but Ann kept yelling anyway. "Matt's not company anymore," she declared, "so he may as well get used to us."

Roz passed the dishes around the table, starting with the roast and the rice casserole.

"I love this rice," Gus said. "It's my favorite dish."

"It was your grandmother's recipe," Roz said. Sweet Gus. With his swimmer's haircut he looked so nice and clean-cut next to Matt, who, now that she thought about it, was the spitting image of Charles Manson. It occurred to her that she might ask him about it—was he trying to look like Manson? Was it a kind of look, like wearing a Nehru jacket?

Gus handed the casserole to Matt, who helped himself to a healthy spoon full, and then Gus passed him the meat. Matt looked down at the meat without taking any. "I don't recognize this cut of beef. What is it?"

"It's a rump roast," Roz said. "It's very tender."

Matt took several slices. "Rump roast. I'm sure it's great, so I'll just try not to think about what it is."

Elaine smiled. "Matt's thinking of becoming a vegetarian."

Ann said, "So what is there to think about?"

Matt said, "Well, to start, whether I want to eat a rump or not. I mean, they didn't hold back on naming that piece of meat."

"I know I want to eat a rump!" Nick said, trying to be funny. Roz glared at him. "Of beef I mean. Or rather cow. Rump of cow."

"Matt and I have both been talking about becoming vegetarians," Elaine said. "Just think about the cow we're eating. Do you think any of us could actually kill a cow? Go out in a field and shoot one?"

"That's not how it's done, Laney," Matt said. "Nobody goes out and shoots a cow in a pasture."

Roz was beginning to feel a bit fuzzy-headed. She'd switched from gin to water—maybe that was the problem, so she got up from the table and went to the kitchen to change back to gin.

Elaine forked a slice of meat onto her plate and passed the platter to Ann, who didn't seem interested in eating. She was grinning at Matt. "What did you just call my sister—*Laney*?"

Nick jumped in. "I bet you don't know Elaine's real name, do you Matt?"

Matt said, "I think I do." He took Elaine's hand. "Her name is Margaret Elaine."

"Yes," Elaine said, "but it's really not Elaine, it's Eleni. E-L-E-N-I. It's Greek. I always have to spell it for people who ask my given name."

Nick winked. "It means flower."

"It also means elope," Gus added. "The verb. To elope."

"Thanks Gus," Elaine said. "Thanks for the info."

"You might consider it," Ann said. "Eloping is a lot faster than getting married."

"Eloping *is* getting married," Roz said as she walked back to the table. She swirled the ice in her glass. "It's just running away to do it. You go off on your own without asking anybody's blessing."

"Well, in the Cherokee tradition, a woman can't marry a member of her tribe," Matt said. "She has to go outside her tribe. Same with the man."

"That doesn't make sense," Gus said. He had tucked his napkin under his chin, an old man's habit Roz could never put her finger on. "So what does a Cherokee do then, get on a horse and look for a woman who's a Sioux?"

"No, no, the Cherokee are not considered a tribe, they're a nation. A tribe is like a clan. So a Cherokee man looks for someone who's not in his clan. He can't marry within his clan, and she can't marry in hers."

"Why are we all of a sudden talking about Cherokees?" Roz said.

"Because I'm one," Matt said. "I'm part Cherokee."

"Really? How so?"

"On my grandmother's side."

"All right," Ann said, "so if you marry Elaine, she'll be part Greek and part Cherokee."

Roz looked closely at Matt. He was too pale to be an Indian, and he didn't have the necessary facial structure. Instead he was round-faced and rather plain, just a brown-haired kid with frizzy hair, a bad complexion and a sweet odor in his clothes that probably came from smoking marijuana. An only child, too. An only child from some little town on the borderline between West Virginia and Tennessee with an electrician for a father and a mother who worked in a nursing home. If she remembered correctly, the two of them owned a camper that they took all their vacations in. They were that kind of family. Nothing remotely Cherokee about them.

She took a swallow of her drink. "Can we finally stop talking about marriage?"

Nick pointed his fork at Matt, waving a bite of meat. "I don't know anything about Cherokees, but it's the opposite with Greeks. You better believe we marry in our clan! That's why it was so hard for me to marry Roz. My mother nearly disowned me when I told her I was dating a girl who isn't Greek. You would've thought I was dating a black girl."

"Good lord, Dad, what did you just say?" Ann said.

Roz felt herself grow warm. It was as if she was being wrapped in an electric blanket. She began to perspire; beads of sweat rolled down her temple and into her hair. Through a film of heat she stared at Nick and his stupid, fifty-year-old, owl-eyed face. Oh, the hardship he'd experienced, marrying an ordinary Baptist from a little small town! All these years, and he'd never told her how hard. She supposed she should be honored that he took such a risk for her, but that's not how it was—it was she who'd taken the risk, not him. It was she who'd abandoned her sad little family, leaving her mother behind in Cumberland so she could go off and marry a Greek man in a Greek church where hardly a word of English was spoken in the ceremony. It was she who'd joined a foreign clan, naming her children Eleni and Antheia and Constantine. And like every good Greek wife, she'd deferred to his mother in nearly everything, knowing— because this is the way of the world—that of the two mothers, hers and Nick's, it would probably be hers who would die first, leaving her feeling fully orphaned (she'd never expressed this, not even to Nick) because she'd never really known her father and because her mother, Margie Grass, while conservative, was neither strong nor a person of good habits (her cigarette smoking, her late nights with her middle-aged boyfriend Artie Fishwick, who was fond of martinis). "I know how it sounds," Nick was saying, "but you have to understand Greek culture."

"Okay, I get where you're coming from," Matt said, "but I don't see anything wrong with miscegenation."

"What's that?" Gus said.

"Miscegenation. It's interracial breeding."

Ann raised her eyebrows. "Breeding? Are we really talking about breeding now?"

"Hold on, that's just the definition of the word," Matt said. "Or maybe it's the clinical definition. It just means interracial dating and marriage."

"Which wouldn't have been tolerated in my family," Nick said.

Ann pushed back from the table and stood up. "I don't think I even know you bigoted people. I'm out of here."

Roz said, "No you don't. You haven't eaten a thing."

Ann sat back down. "Okay, so if I have to stay for this conversation, I can tell you right now that I don't see what difference it makes what race you are, it just matters that you love each other. So Elaine, if you and Matt get married, you'll be a big old mix of Greek and German and Cherokee and whatever else you are, Matt. English most likely, and that will be just fine with me."

"No doubt there'd be African in there too, way back," Matt said. "I think we'd all be surprised how mixed we are. We just don't know it."

Elaine said, "Well to be correct, it's not me that would be a mix of Cherokee and English and Greek and all that. It would be our children, right Matt?"

Roz began to feel as if she were sliding into a hole. How had they gotten here? Was it all because Nick had married out of his "clan"? Where did that come from? Why did he always have to be so damned insulting? The room was growing dim as smoke, and while she was surrounded by voices, she felt herself fading away. Talk, talk, talk…the broken record of Matt Duckworth and the rest of the Nicolaides family…talk, talk, talk…while she faded into the background, a mute shadow at her end of the table. She willed herself to focus. She looked at her children, one by one: Ann, now entering the ripeness of late adolescence, too sexy for her own good; Gus, shy and dark and wide-eyed; and Elaine, so lovely, with a genuine look in her face, as if she believed in all good things. Yes, she'd given birth to each of them—amazing to think that without her, they wouldn't be here at all! Instead they'd be little unformed specks in space still waiting for someone to bring them into the world. She looked at Matt and tried to imagine him as a baby. His mother, whatever her name was (Dorothy? Bertha?) had done her part too, bringing little Matthew wiggling to life. She felt a sudden affection for him. He might have actually been cute. It was too bad his mom couldn't have given him a sibling.

"Matt, how have you liked being an only child?" she said.

Elaine whipped around in her seat. "What? What did you say? That Matt's an only child?"

Roz could feel everyone look at her. "Sorry. I guess I was just thinking about Matt—you know, what it's like to be an only child." She smiled weakly at him. "I was one, too."

"Well that's completely changing the subject!" Elaine said. "Here we'd just begun talking about Vietnam, and where were you? Did you just totally check out on us? She looked over at Matt. "And who says Matt's an only child? Where'd you get that idea?"

Matt held up his hand. "Whoa, whoa, Laney. Technically I am. I mean, I guess you could say I'm an only child." He looked at Roz. "It's a long story. I do have a brother, but he had to be sent away. His name is George."

"That's my brother's name too!" Nick said.

Ann said, "All right, that's it, I'm out of here." She slid back her chair and left the room, which gave Gus permission to go too. He folded his napkin and set it next to his plate, and then he was gone.

Elaine said, "See, Mom? You ought not to go making assumptions. You don't know what you're talking about. You can't just go off half-cocked and say stuff you don't know."

Nick said, "I agree, we all need to listen better." He took a last bite and gave Roz a hard look. "You have to admit that was out of the blue. We were just talking about Vietnam, and Matt was telling us about what it takes to be a conscientious objector, which you know I don't agree with, not the least bit, and you blurt out something about only children."

"It's Okay," Matt said, his voice turning smooth all of a sudden. He looked over at Roz. "I think it's hard being an only child."

Roz met his eyes. They were blue. Not clear blue, but a sort of sweet, watery, gray blue.

"The war's over," she said.

"What?" Nick said. "Have you gone completely insane?"

She decided to ignore him, although deep inside she felt like slapping his face. "It's in the paper today. This is the official end of the Vietnam War."

"That's amazing," Matt said. "You'd think there'd be fireworks or something."

"Well that war was already pretty much over," Nick said. "We lost. That's all you can conclude. It's a crying shame. We should've bombed them back to the Stone Age."

"What? Bomb them?" Roz said.

"Man," Matt said, "whoa. Looks like we're on opposite sides on this one. Maybe we should just stick to a safe topic, like art." He turned to Roz. "How's the paper snipping coming along?"

"Scherenschnitte," she said.

"I know, sorry," Matt said. "I can never remember what it's called."

"Neither can I," Nick said, laughing. "When she says it, she sounds like she's just sneezed. I don't know why they just don't call it paper-cutting."

Roz glared at him. "The same reason we don't call you a drug dispenser. A pill counter, a prescription filler."

Nick glanced over at Matt and smiled. "She gets touchy about her hobby. But I say if it makes her happy, it's a good thing. Roz has been so much more content now that she has something to do with her time."

Feeling a sudden clarity, Roz rose from her chair. At least Matt had asked about her art. At least he had a semblance of understanding of what it means to try to make something, to produce something with one's own hands. And if Matt wasn't an actual only child, he was as good as being one, seeing as how his poor brother had to be sent away.

"Wait right there, Matt," she said, "I have something to give you."

She left the dining room and walked unsteadily through the

kitchen, where the roasting pan sat on the stove, congealed beef fat clinging to the sides in an orange ring. She caught sight of it and kept going. Down the hall, up the stairs, past the closed door of Elaine's room, the cracked door of Gus's room, the closed door of Ann's. What she'd give Matt was one of her works of art, whether he really appreciated it or not. It wouldn't be the traditional depiction of a household, with the husband and wife and their cows and chickens, and it wouldn't be Noah's Ark, either. Instead she'd give him "The Intricate Heart." It was something she'd created especially for Nick last year, but he'd never framed it, and after a while he'd forgotten she'd even given it to him. He'd left it on the coffee table for days, and if it hadn't been for her quick hands, somebody would've used it as a placemat.

She dug through her drawer of cuttings and pulled out the heart. It was a fine work of art, no matter what anybody said. How dare Nick reject it—because not caring about a gift was the same as rejecting it, was it not? She tucked the crisp paper, so finely cut, beneath her arm. Now it would belong to Matt: that would serve Nick right. For that matter, Matt could have all her work, every piece. She could toss them onto the table. Feminine art, like lace.

But on her way downstairs she was stopped by a cat's cry. Punky seemed to be trapped on the balcony. She went to the balcony door and opened it, only to find bed sheets tied to the rail. Ann's contraption. So that's how she'd run away so many times. Roz couldn't believe she hadn't figured it out till now. Ann was probably running loose at that very moment, but who could blame her? When Roz was a girl, running was her main dream. She'd wake in the morning in the little house she shared with her mother, step out onto the porch, and confront gray mountains. When she finally did move away, what she got was only Nick. Smug, self-satisfied Nick Nicolaides. And their children.

She stepped into the pile of sheets. No wonder Ann had fled: if she could run away herself, if she had somewhere to go, she'd flee too. And wouldn't Nick just bust, to see that his wife had left him. And wouldn't he be helpless, not knowing how to care for himself, because he'd never had to.

The sheets trembled at her feet. Punky was trying to climb up. Poor cat. He was so slow, fifteen years old now, but she loved him. He'd become her only confidante. It was crazy but true. She drove him in her car whenever he hopped in, and she held him in her arms in bed when Nick stayed late at the pharmacy. Punky was warm and quiet. He purred, he listened. Now he was clawing his way up. She could hear the bed sheets rip, a satisfying sound. She dropped her artwork to the floor and reached over the rail to help him, pulling up the bed sheets arm over arm as if Punky were a fat fish on a line. Amazingly, he didn't let go.

Dusk fell. The trees in the yard were silhouetted against a gloaming sky. With Punky safe on the balcony, Roz sat down and let him curl in her lap. Here they were. For a moment she forgot how she got here, how she came to be upstairs in the first place. It was nice to be alone. The only thing missing was a cigarette. She set Punky down and went inside to get her cigarettes and lighter from the top of her dresser. Cigarettes, lighter, ashtray, and, leaning against the mirror, a photograph of herself and Nick when they were young. How beautiful he looked back then in his tuxedo, lean, loose, and smiling. If he looked like that now, she'd probably submit to him again. But that man was long gone.

She went back out to the balcony and lit a cigarette. So they'd had another failed family gathering. Whose fault was it? Nick would say it was hers—it was always her fault. Slowly the dinner came back to her, the conversation playing out in her mind like a bad movie. *You better believe it was hard for me to marry Roz!* By now Nick had probably poured himself an after-dinner Scotch, and he was sitting at the table with his empty plate in front of him, holding forth. *Let me tell you, Matt.* And where was Elaine? Probably clearing the table, good girl, pretending to be married. *More content now that she has something to do with her time.*

Roz's heart began to race a little. She dug her cigarette into the folds of the bed sheets and watched a burning hole take shape. If only she could start a fire, she'd be forced to jump. Down below, Nick would look out the window and watch her hit the ground. Boom, what a mess. She gathered her artwork and began to toss each one overboard, the Pied Piper, Noah's Ark, the Family Tree. Here you go, take my love. With tiny scissors, so sharp that she had to be careful not to nip her skin, she'd meticulously cut the equivalent of air: the air surrounding a dove on a tree limb, the air around the limb itself, the air between thin blades of grass. Last of all was The Intricate Heart. She took it between her fingers and let it float.

The bed sheets began to smolder, giving off the brown, satisfying odor of scorched fabric. Punky stood up and went to the door to be let inside, but Roz wouldn't budge. She lowered herself against the wall and watched to see if Nick might emerge from down below. Out in the yard, hornets crawled within their nest, layer upon layer of paper manufactured by their queen. Perhaps the smell of smoke would draw them out. At last the back door opened, and the two men ran into the yard like dogs. "Something's on fire!" Matt cried. She pulled Punky close. What she wouldn't give for a rock to throw now, a missile to aim straight at the hornet nest. Out from their little hole the hornets would fly, ready to sting, and she wouldn't say a word. Not one. Instead she'd hold her tongue and wait to see what would happen next. Up on the burning balcony, she and Punky, the innocent ones.

CHURCH RETREAT, 1975

After a long walk the two girls, named Lib and Jenny, began to get hot and sweaty, their sunburned faces dripping, so they took to walking in the ocean up to their knees. It was the first Saturday in April, so the water was still very cold, but after a while even the water didn't cool them down. They began talking of going all the way in. The beach was deserted at the north end, just one old motel, so no one would see.

"Let's swim in our clothes," Lib said, "it'll be fun."

She grabbed Jenny's hand, and they ran squealing into the first set of waves, their skin suddenly goose-bumped, their hearts pounding. Lib lifted Jenny's arm as they leapt together over a rough wave, then she lowered her down again, forcing her briefly under. Jenny came up sputtering, laughing, and they both went under—they were fully in now—so they let the water come up to their necks, their hair floating.

Soon Jenny began to complain that her shorts had stuck to her thighs, she wanted to undress. She stood and began unzipping, pushing her shorts down over her ankles, and then she pulled her t-shirt over her head. The cold sea slapped her nude belly. Lib squirmed out of her clothes too, keeping on her bra and panties, and she waved her t-shirt like a flag.

Back down the beach, where the rest of the church group lay sunning themselves and listening to a radio, no one missed them. They'd had breakfast followed by a devotional, and now it was free time.

A PATROL OF BROWN pelicans flew low over the ocean. From where he stood behind the glass door to his motel room, Davie Ellis watched them. Big brown birds. He blinked hard. Hueys coming in, a nine-ship lift in the jungle heat. He blinked again. Birds first, then choppers, then birds. He pulled back the door to his room, stepped out into the sand and saw: girls.

On the golf course earlier, the sun had burned his retina, leaving a fiery orange blot in his eye every time he blinked. He'd tried to see through the blot long enough to hit the ball down the fairway, but the more he blinked, the brighter the blot became. When the pin flag became a flare, he knew he was still a sick man. Even a golf vacation was fucking Vietnam.

The two girls were waving something. He should call his buddy Ned, now mixing drinks, but he didn't want to share this. Not yet, anyway: the pale white skin, the wet long hair, the slender waving arms. He stepped back into the room to pour tequila over the melting ice in his glass. He gulped it down.

Out in the ocean, Jenny had had enough of swimming. "Oh gosh," she said, "oh gosh, I'm freezing!" Lib looked at her and took her hand. "Your lips are blue, let's get out." They splashed onto the beach, where the cold air hit them.

Ned appeared at Davie's room door grinning like a fool. He held a plastic pitcher in his hand. His own poison. "Jug monkey!"

Davie ignored him and kept watching the girls, who now stood face to face on the beach.

"Dang," Ned said.

Davie felt himself reel.

"They're almost naked."

Davie took the pitcher from Ned's hand, the odor of Evercleer and grape juice filling his nostrils. Hoping to clear his mind, he tilted the pitcher and drank.

Ned grinned. "What those girls need is a towel."

Davie watched him go to the bathroom and bring out two skimpy white towels. Then he watched him head out toward the beach. Yellow shorts, madras shirt, thin calves, a bald patch.

He tilted the pitcher again and felt the jug monkey burn. Outside on the first dune sea oats swayed. Through blurry eyes he saw himself humping through swamp grass over a flattened trail. The air conditioning unit revved up: mortar fire.

Here came the girls. Somehow, between Ned taking them the towels and their walk to the motel, they'd slipped their wet clothes back on, everything see-through.

"Look what the cat brought in!" Ned proclaimed. "It's party time."

Davie bit his lip and smiled, and the girls half-smiled back. Shy or maybe afraid. And so young. When Ned held out his arm to show them into the room, they ducked as if entering a tent.

At this, Davie was a goner, shit-scared and running back to the rotten hooch the platoon passed a half-hour ago, escaping mortar rounds. He ducked into the dark doorway, his M-16 out in front of him, and found a girl. By herself, just this one girl. She opened her mouth to scream, but instead of shooting he shoved her against the thatched wall. Then he fell on her.

"WANT A LITTLE DRINK?" Ned led one of the girls over to the sink, his hand low on her back. She walked warily, whispering a name. "Lib?"

What happened next in the hooch he could never allow himself to see. It was a blot in his vision he'd put there himself.

Suddenly the room announced itself to him: nubby polyester bedspreads, yellowed sheets, a banged-up Motorola TV suspended from the ceiling so no one could steal it. And standing next to the door, muttering to herself, a pretty girl dressed in wet shorts and a clinging t-shirt, barefooted. A thoroughly American girl, and he had not touched her. At this, he began to sob.

Later that night, the girls would say it was prayer that saved them from the men. One of the men began to cry for some reason. It was a miracle. God had intervened.

HONEST AND TRUE

The first time Walter laid a hand on Lacy, really laid a hand on her, it was a Saturday in April, the bees out already, gnats in the eyes, and all the world full of sunlight and color. She had forced him to go looking for her in the rising heat of the afternoon. He hadn't dressed right, he'd even worn his leather jacket, which he was forced to carry under his arm. His hands were damp from sweat; even his legs were damp, as if he'd just come from a swim in his clothes, and his head was beginning to ache at the temples.

He would not have been walking in the heat, but Lacy had slithered out in the morning like a snake. When he rose, he stepped into the front room and looked out the picture window at the greening onions and grass, and he saw, at the bottom of the hill along the curb, the empty space where his car should have been.

Nothing moved. He looked for his little dog Buck. He clapped his hands, but the dog did not come. He clapped again and again, watching for his dog to come leaping through the doorway, open mouth and long pink tongue. If Buck would come, he could rub his hand across the dog's stiff coat. And he would worry less.

But there was no Buck. And no Lacy. She had left him so often that he'd grown accustomed to feeling for her in the morning, reaching across the bed only to touch the cool surface of the mattress in his flat hand. Sometimes she would come back smoking. I was out, she'd say, so I had to run up to the store and get some. Perhaps she also had a little paper bag, like proof. Doughnuts, gum.

But this was the first time she had taken the dog with her, if that's where Buck was now. Walter stood watching the window for a long time to see Buck appear, nose to the ground, tail high in the air. But Buck did not show, and the sun filled everything with empty, hot light. Walter took the extra house key from the hook by the door, since Lacy had taken his real set of keys, the car keys and the garage key and the rest. And he set out on foot in search of her and his dog.

It was hot and the air was still. He crossed Peace Street at the big intersection and headed down Hill Street, past the bank with cars in line at the drive-in window and the house with antiques for sale in the driveway, the high-backed chairs and black cauldrons buried in the ivy, dusty rolled rugs and tables littered with china and glass. No one guarded the stuff. So it had been easy, back in the fall when he first met Lacy, to slip a glass teardrop from a chandelier and tuck it into his pocket as a gift for her. The way it reflected light, it was like a diamond. If he could have put it on her finger, he would have.

Because she was so beautiful, and she was his. He loved her long brown hair with its light streaks bleached by the sun. Her thin body and her creamy smooth skin. And her hands, the way she talked to him: he loved the way she could wave whole worlds in the air with her fingers, the stars and the moon and all the twinkling universe. How he loved her, his Lacy.

And how she teased him. His heart ached to think of it now, how hot and alone he was, again. Chasing after her, again. He saw her flick her long hair, saw her turn her smooth, pale neck. Saw her teasing eyes. And her mouth, which, if he could catch her fast enough, he would kiss into submission.

Cars passed by. So much traffic for an early Saturday afternoon. Lacy could be anywhere. Since when did he start giving her the car? She drove recklessly, shoving the stick into gear. Her painted fingernails gripped the wheel, dug crescents into the leather cover he'd laced on. A custom job, like everything on the car. The exhaust system—custom. The high suspension—custom. Everything custom, everything top quality, he'd seen to it. And then turned it over to Lacy.

At the shopping center, he entered the bottom level of the parking deck and took the narrow sidewalk next to the building. A group of teenagers approached him. The girls wore little tee shirts cropped over their bare bellies, beautiful sweet navels and newly tanned skin. When they passed him, a sweet scent of fruit overcame him—their hair, their clothing—and heat rose on his chest like steam.

He could feel the shiver of cars on the deck overhead. Everywhere, there were cars, pulling in and out, moving in a swarm in the gray light of the deck, and he wondered for an instant if this might be a holiday. There could be a party going on today, and Lacy could already be there. He felt hollow to think of it. Then something caught his eye, something leaping. He turned to see the white flash of Buck's face as he leapt against a car window—his own car, parked in a corner by the stairwell. Buck threw his paws against the window, clawing his way to the top of the glass and biting at the thin slot of air Lacy had left for him. Walter rushed across the lot, and the feeling came to him that the car, with Buck inside, had been there a long time.

Buck clawed his way to the top of the window and thrust his nose in the crevice. Walter pressed his fingers into the space and let Buck chew his knuckles. The glass was wet from the dog's panting tongue, and the black leather upholstery glistened with coarse white fur. As Buck leapt from one window to another, following Walter, he stepped again and again over the things Lacy had left in the car—her soft, stained makeup bag, her hairbrush, a pair of jeans, and her book, *The Art of Bonsai*. It was the ripping cover of the book that now caught Walter's eye, how a gash opened wider each time Buck raced back and forth. The dog's claws tore into the photograph of the tiny, perfect maple tree on the cover. Walter could almost feel the dog's sharp nails as they scratched into the paper, and it gave him a perverse pleasure. Go on, he thought, tear it up. Tear it completely up.

Cars passing through the deck slowed as they approached, and faces peered from the windows to see him leaning, half twisted, against his car. He was so hot by now that his shirt was soaked, but what he felt was not heat or thirst but the dead weight of jealousy. In time, Lacy would return. Someone, some man, would pull up in a car, the passenger door would open, and Lacy would hop out, lightning-quick, smiling, tilting her head to say goodbye.

Two blocks up Peace Street was a Texaco station, and a friend he knew. With a black heart he left his dog and his car and began walking again, jacket in hand, out into the blinding sunlight. To get the tools he needed.

SHE HAD NOT INTENDED to leave him for so long. *Honest,* she would say to him later, *I am honest, I am true.* He had the day off, a rare thing. And it was a Saturday in spring, bright and hot, like summer. So why would she leave him on such a day of opportunity? They could drive out to Reedy Creek Park, watch Buck chase squirrels in the woods. Or they could buy some beer and head out toward the coast, just drive and drive and see where they would end up.

They had done it once. Made it all the way to Atlantic Beach in just over two hours, the radio blasting. She had danced in her seat, and he had watched her appreciatively, slapping time on the steering wheel.

No, she had intended just to go out a little while, because the weather was so warm and the smell of flowers was in the air, there were birds going on and on, singing, rustling in the branches of the bush outside their window. He had not heard any of it, she knew. But the smell of flowers—that was enough to wake anyone, wasn't it? It was like perfume in the air, like honey! And when the neighbors started up their lawn mower, you couldn't stay in bed another minute.

But he'd kept on sleeping, mouth open, his body curled in a ball with the sheets between his knees. She lifted the window shade, but he didn't wake. She shoved a drawer closed when she got out her jeans. Still he slept. So she took his keys and slipped out of the house. When Buck followed her and jumped into the back seat, she didn't force him out. Instead she gave him a pat on the head as he jumped to the front, his paws wet with dew.

The morning air was breezy and damp, as if everything had

just been washed. Lacy rolled down a window and let her hair blow, and Buck lifted his nose into the breeze. Some kids had set up a car wash at the Texaco on Peace Street; two girls raised a sign, giggling. They wore little frayed shorts and sneakers.

One thing leads to another, she would tell Walter, life happens. So the smell of flowers started it—what was it, wisteria? Honeysuckle on the fence? How could he just lie there in the bed when the day was so bright and sweet and beckoning? So the weather had something to do with it: she'd just had to get up and go outside. And there were those girls washing cars. They bounced on their heels, sang along with a radio. And then the idea to go shopping for shorts, now that the weather was hot enough—the girls gave her the idea. And then, and then….How much could she tell him?

The voice she heard in the store at the shopping center, the deep voice she recognized. Lacy, he said. *Lacy?* She'd answered, *Tom?* They hadn't seen each other in years, since they were in high school, yet here they were, together again, and it seemed like time suddenly became visible, like a curtain opening on a stage, and the years peeled back. While they talked, she held the bag containing her new shorts under one arm and jingled the car keys. He suggested they go get lunch, maybe take a drive, so she went to Walter's car and slipped into the back seat, Buck jumping, to change out of her jeans. And locked the car and left.

There was so much Walter could never understand, even if she could tell him in long, long sentences, in paragraphs, in pages. How it feels to be back in a strange car once again, like being on a first date. Looking at the dashboard, the things hanging from the mirror, all new and different. And looking over at a man's hands on the wheel, the veins in his hands, his strong wrists. And being with him, just being with him, the new feeling of a different man.

No, not all that. Only the feeling of being with Tom Daniels, someone she once knew very well, the two of them skipping out of school for their own personal field trip to Durham, to the Eno River.

The feeling of loud conversation, it was like yelling and screaming compared to life with Walter! Music playing, full volume, and tons of talk.

Could he know what she meant?

Where to? Tom started the motor. She settled back, slipped off her shoes. She let him look at her without looking back. *The Eno*, she said. So they wound their way out of town, the sun sliding higher in the sky. They listened to music, found with no surprise that they still shared the same tastes. It was Lacy who liked the volume higher, who turned on Pink Floyd until the floorboard shook, and she sang *breathe, breathe in the air* and then Tom sang *don't be afraid to care.* But then she stopped, hearing Tom's voice above everything, its low, awkward sound, off-key, and she felt embarrassed for him all of a sudden, and a regret, however momentary, that she'd come in the car with him in the first place. She thought briefly of Buck back in the car, the windows rolled—she should have given him more air—and she thought of Walter at home, alone. He would be looking for her by now. But then she let the feeling pass. She rolled the window down, and cool air blew across her face.

I have an idea, she shouted. Let's get a picnic! Bread and cheese and wine!

Tom grinned and shouted back to her. A beef stick! It was the kind of silly joke she loved. A beef stick and a cheese log!

she said, laughing. Pickles, salami, liver loaf! he continued. Head cheese and bratwurst and pink pickled eggs! she added, and she dropped her head back against the seat and laughed, hard. Then she reached over and touched his knee.

At the river the trees hung down over the water in places, and it was cool under there. Tom took Lacy's hand and led her over the rocky bank to the water's edge, and it all came back—how they used to walk along until they found a little cove where the bank evened out and formed a kind of beach beneath the trees, how they would slip down unseen and put their bare feet in the water and spend the hours alone. On a spring day like this they might bring some weed and a bottle of cheap wine that they could keep chilled in the shallow water, and they would smoke and drink the wine slowly until they grew silly and numb. Then they would play little touching games, caressing each other with slow fingers and long kisses, but Lacy would always stop short and Tom would grow angry and sullen until she began to kiss him again, teasing him with her tongue but always finishing with a vague, deflating no. Maybe next time.

Now, once again, they brought wine, and they found their place against the bank. Tom pulled a Swiss knife from his pocket and twisted open the cork, while Lacy watched him closely—his small, almost tender hand gripping the neck of the bottle, his fingers squeezing the knife. He offered her the first swallow, and she took the bottle and drank, knowing he was watching her too.

If Walter could see them, if by some magic he hovered nearby, floating, like a moth or one of the dragonflies that hovered flat-winged over the water, he would be furious. Because they looked so comfortable—Lacy was aware of this, as if there were a mirror at her back—and the spring air was light but very warm, and the river was narrow, like a creek, and the water swirled silently in circles around the rocks. And the wine: if Walter could taste it, he could feel how well it lost its bitter dustiness with each swallow, how it became soft and almost sweet on the tongue.

But Walter was not here, of course, it was Tom instead. He wanted to know everything about her, so she told him about college, how she enrolled and dropped out twice before finishing, and she told him about all the people she had known back then, their long weekend trips to the mountains, the big camping parties with rows of tents and cars parked beneath the trees, people coming and going and you never knew exactly who they all were. One of those friends was almost deaf—she had less than a quarter of the hearing of a hearing person—and so Lacy had learned to sign. Finger-spelling at first, then words and idioms and syntax.

Sign language, Tom said. Show me some signs. So she let her fingers fly, all the while keeping her face still. I—happy—see—you—again. This spring day—beautiful. This wine—very nice. This river—very nice also.

But she did not tell him about Walter.

How he'd captivated her one Saturday night in the fall, climbed in the back seat of the car and took her hand and then took the rest of her, silently, and she let him. How she would have sold her soul for him—had nearly sold her name and her birthright, since her parents would hear nothing of it, this body-builder, this muscle man with grease beneath his fingernails. He's so common, they said, and so defiant. Which meant he didn't know how to behave like a gentleman when in their presence, didn't even know how to dress. Or talk. Because of all things, he was deaf. In response, she eased herself beneath him in the darkness, and she smothered his neck with kisses. And then she listened with delight to the odd noises that rose from his throat. He groaned non-words, speaking sounds he thought he remembered as a little boy, his leftover language.

How could she tell someone like Tom about Walter? She watched him on the riverbank and felt contempt mixed with desire. He seemed delicate, the way he lifted the wine to his mouth with one hand, tilting the bottle back, pressing his lips over the rim. Across his face there was the faintest shadow of his shaved beard, which Lacy could not resist—she had to touch it, to draw the back of her forefinger across his cheek and ask him, are your whiskers really blonde?

She drew a finger across, felt the fine stubble, more fine and soft than Walter's. Everything about Tom was softer than Walter, so Lacy wanted to peel down his shirt at the collar and feel the softness of his throat and chest, which she still remembered from years past, flat and smooth like a boy's.

Where did you meet Walter? he wanted to know.

Lacy sat up. She looked down between her knees and saw green, swimming moss and the frayed root of a tree. So he knew about Walter after all—everybody knew about Walter. Driving his red Camaro with the bass up high, thumping through the city with his windows down, dangerous, loud, a thick shock of hair falling over one brow, his big shoulders behind the wheel. And deaf. God, you just couldn't believe he was deaf, with all the noise he made. Could, but wouldn't, beat the crap out of anybody who said a word about his being deaf. Could be the first to *detect* it if anybody said a single, solitary word.

Lacy sat next to Tom but felt Walter more, felt herself

claimed by him, so she eased closer to Tom anyway, like a dare. He looked out over the river. When he tilted the bottle to his mouth, she watched the muscle in his jaw. She leaned a knee against his knee. He offered her the wine, and she drank deeply.

Tell me about Walter, he said, and Lacy closed her eyes. There's nothing to tell, she said, he's just a little crazy. Tom's skin pressed against her skin—his knee and her thigh. She took another swallow. It's hot here in the sun, she said, so he placed a hand on her back and led her to their old cove beneath the trees. There, in the shade, while she let Tom unbutton her shorts and begin to touch her, she thought about Walter. First she was back in their room with all his things, his boots and clothes on the floor, the stray coins on the dresser and the little leather Bible he kept by the bed like a good-luck charm. Then it was that first night again, that Saturday back in September when she met him at that dull party her agency had put on, with the sign interpreters and the few deaf people, the low music half the room could not even hear, and the plates of little sandwiches and small talk, all in sign except the hearing people who talked and signed at the same time. When Walter arrived, he stepped into the room as if he'd come to press charges.

So many times she went back to that night, her one best night, so sweet and scary you could have made it into a movie: Walter stepping into the room, silent, bigger and rougher than everybody, looking straight into her face—could he see through her?—and when she finally met him, walking around the dining table where the food was laid out, she signed to him, telling him her name and asking his name and where he worked. And he signed back to her, just enough and no more.

How quiet he was then, and how different—he and his friend

Rob Zimmerman, a deaf guy she'd also never seen or heard of—how much younger, and better, than all the others. So she went with them when they left the party, followed a few steps behind, watching as they signed to each other, and she listened, amazed, as Walter spoke in his low voice, in wide-mouthed sounds, like animal speech. She rode in the back seat of the car, Walter driving, and watched the two men as they rode together in the front. Walter laughed often, signing with his one free hand. They stopped for beer. And when they all went back to the car, Walter surprised her by giving his keys to his friend and climbing into the back seat with her.

She could relive the moment at will. He climbed into the back seat without saying a word, and his friend started the engine and they pulled away, the radio going, and then he swept his arm across her shoulder as if he meant to own her, and so before the night was over, he did.

Now Lacy kissed Tom, feeling the newness of a different mouth, and she lifted both hands to caress his different face. He was small and tight and blonde, unlike Walter, and he was too eager, also unlike Walter—as if they had to hurry before the crowds came, picnickers with their packs and radios and canoes. The river was quiet and muddy. Blackbirds pecked along the rocks. What's the rush, Lacy said in a blurry voice, and Tom drew his hands back from beneath her hips. It's Okay, she told him, and then she coached him, pulling him in, letting him lose himself there on the bank of the Eno River, doing what she'd never allowed herself to do in those afternoons back in high school, when they liked to skip out, playing hooky.

~~~

THE HOUSE WHERE THEY lived was a house to watch, set up on its little hill halfway down Vass Avenue, the red car parked in front. "The deaf man's house," the neighbors called it. Or "that body-builder's house," since on warm days Walter took his weights to the front walkway and lifted, bare-chested. He liked to meet his friends outside and stand in the grass, talking, vocalizing and signing at the same time. All the while his neighbors looked out from their porches and watched, fascinated, or else they stopped at their windows and gazed. Then one day Lacy appeared, a small, pretty woman wearing jeans and a smooth suede jacket, her hair down her back. And then she moved in with him, carrying dresses in suit bags and a pair of finches in a cage. Even after she had been there a long time, she was something to watch, quick in the house and quick out. And never ashamed to wrap her arms around Walter's thick bare waist.

Now a shadow fell over the house, the afternoon shadow that always darkened one side of the street and cooled it down. Walter drove up with his little dog perched on his lap. He parked next to the curb, opened the door, and let the dog jump into the grass. Something was amiss. He left the motor running as he stepped out of the car and took long strides up the hill to his house. He threw open the front door, leaving a clear view into the dark hallway, and called in a loud voice—Lacy!

So often the noises that came from that house could make you shiver. Sometimes it was a low bark, an almost inhuman sound. Sometimes a pounding on the floor. Sometimes shrill laughter, and then abrupt, bare silence. In the glow of the lights in the front room, dark figures passed in pantomime. Or else there would be loud music, so loud that you went to your windows and shut them, to muffle the thrumming bass. Then sometimes, little parties. People would gather in the yard, gesturing to one another, talking in sign with their scooping arms and flat palms cutting and layering the air.

Sometimes Walter's mother would come. She drove a white Mercury Cougar with peeling bumper stickers on the back bumper. BETHEL BIBLEWAY WELCOMES YOU and JESUS IS THE TRUTH AND THE LIGHT. When she opened the door and eased herself from the car, she wore her body like a drooping heavy coat, she was so rumpled and rolled at the joints, and her face bore the constant grimace of pain. Walter would greet her on the walkway and take her by the elbow, and she would lay a hand on his shoulder and lean on him. They would talk openly, loudly, her voice rising so high that anyone could follow their conversation. "Why haven't you been to visit me?" she would say, and Walter would answer, also loudly, in words only they could understand. "That's no excuse," you could hear her say, "No excuse at all." Their voices roared from within the house, and the door opened just long enough for the dog to be let out into the yard, and then the door closed again. Later, when they emerged from the house and walked down to the car, they would continue their conversation in the open once more, and you could hear fragments. She lowered herself into the car gently, as if she might break something, and reached for her son's face. You could feel that she wanted to touch his hair or his cheek. But she always drew back at the last moment, and she would sink into her seat and turn the key in the ignition to start the old rattling engine. Then Walter would lift the hood and look underneath, leaning into the motor until his jeans fell beneath his waist. "Rev it up!" he would shout—the clearest, most understandable words he could say.

He had a job as a mechanic at one of the big Amoco stations

on Glenwood Avenue, where he worked in one of the bays by himself. He could do any kind of repair work on a car. The other mechanics said Walter simply had the touch, feeling in an engine what he could not hear, although he did hear certain sounds in the low range, like the roar of an engine in high gear. This noise entered his mind through a hollow passageway—he saw it as a finger making an impression on wet clay—and he was seized with pleasure every time it came to him. The other two mechanics in the shop thought it was funny that a deaf man could be so noisy, but his boss, a wiry ex-Marine in his fifties who wore a pink hearing aid in one ear, understood Walter, speaking to him with simple signs and finger-spelling.

Not even his mother could speak to him this way, since she refused to learn sign language. If she spoke to him in sign, she reasoned, then he would never learn to read lips, and the world would be shut off to him. So when he was a boy she forced him to watch her as she spoke, squeezing his little cheekbones with one hand and drawing his gaze upward. Then she forced him to speak back. So he spoke, just for her, loudly, crudely—and while he spoke she focused on him with such intensity that he felt his words take shape in her eyes. But no one else understood him when he talked—he saw this early, before he even entered school for the first time—and people never turned their faces toward him the way his mother did, to let him read their moving lips. In this way Walter became a solitary boy, "deaf and dumb," with the bones of one ear fused at birth and the defective other ear growing more silent with time.

Two things saved him: the loud noise of engines and a little classroom for the hard of hearing. And when he was older, a third thing: a woman's light warm hands.

Beneath the grid of fluorescent light the deaf children sat in a circle in hard school chairs, the teacher in the middle, in performance. Her skirt tossed, her arms swirled in circles, her face radiant with light. She approached them one at a time and touched a mere fingertip beneath their chins, lifting their faces, taking their eyes with her eyes, and then she smacked two fingers against her upturned palm—listen! Walter loved her flying hands and her swooping arms, and he waited breathlessly for her to step to his chair, her skirt whispering at his knees. Then the finger beneath his chin, and the offered warm hand. Years later, when the first girl loved him, speaking to him with her mouth, he wanted to feel her arms around him most of all. He took one hand, then the other, and placed them behind his back., He smiled and pled with his eyes. Just hold me, tight.

But Lacy had spoken to him in sign. "Name—" she had said, "name?" Behind her, in the next room, other party guests sat talking with their hands, a blocky woman wearing something like a kimono, and another woman of similar size with wide, commanding hands, and two men Walter recognized from the agency of sign interpreters and services for the deaf. Lacy spelled her name with her fingers, L-A-C-Y, and Walter thought at first it was a mistake—Lucy? The light of a chandelier shone in her eyes, and he could not stop looking at them. If he had known the word, he would have said later, after she left him the next morning, with one last kiss promising to return, that he had been enchanted.

He had taken her to his house because she'd agreed to go, and they'd sat in his kitchen drinking beer and then bourbon on ice, talking. You are not so good at signing, he told her, laughing— even though you are an interpreter. How do you do it, he wanted to know, when you are so bad at it, and she laughed and said, with my hands and fingers and my friendly smile, and then she told him he was no good at reading lips, either, so he took her face in his hands and kissed her, a long and soft kiss, and he said, *I can read yours.* All night, as they talked and drank and kissed, he felt that she had always belonged here, with him, and he knew he could never stand to let her go. As morning broke and a single bird began to sing outside in the filmy air, the house having turned cold and damp, he led her by the hand to his bedroom and undressed her in silence, watching goosebumps rise on her skin as she stood there, spellbound, watching his hands at work.

It was hard to say who seduced whom, although Walter would always feel that she had seduced him, that she had begun to seduce him from the moment they first met at that party. Her eyes danced, her fingers spoke, and Walter was lost. That night, as they fell onto his bed toward dawn, as she wrapped herself around him because she was cold and naked and ready for him, he could have cried—did cry, in fact, although she never saw the tears that filled the corners of his eyes. He buried himself in her body, and she rose above him and smiled into his face, then settled her chest across his chest, cupping his quiet ears in her hands, the ears his mother once slapped to "shake something loose," and then she bent to kiss his mouth, and then his cheek. *Beautiful,* she said to him in sign, *beautiful you.*

In those early days of fall, as Lacy began to visit Walter more and more, the neighbors would often see them out front. Lacy would drive up in a clean black car, something expensive— perhaps it was a Peugeot, perhaps an Audi. The driver's door would open and her leg would appear first, her boot heel and her jeans, and then the rest of her would emerge, the lean body, the long hair that fell below her shoulders. Often she was smoking a cigarette, which she would place between her teeth while she straightened her clothes with both hands, and then she would toss her leather sack over one shoulder. As she stepped up the walk, the door of the house would open as if by magic, and Walter would appear. He pushed the door back to let her in, and he bent to kiss her forehead as she stepped by him and disappeared within.

If Walter seemed possessed by her, it was because he was so ready at the door with a kiss, his upreaching hand behind her back. Once, when she did not come to his door as he expected, he sat in his room until the wee hours of morning, curled beneath the small pale light of a single lamp, reading his Bible. It was the part about the man and wife he was after, some phrase he had seen as a young man, once he'd finally learned to read—*for this cause shall a man leave father and mother, and shall cleave to his wife and the twain shall be one flesh.* When she was gone, he felt what it meant to cleave. He would cleave with all he had—cleave, cling, hold Lacy until she became his wife in all but name (and in name, too, if she would surrender that much, if her father would surrender that much), and he would leave his mother (his own father having left her, long ago)—and live with Lacy forever.

Now she was gone again. But he saw her everywhere. There was her coffee cup on the kitchen counter, half-filled, the cream gathered in a circle at the top; and on the couch in the living room, tossed carelessly, there were so many clothes—the silvery satin camisole she'd worn to bed, the sweater from yesterday, the little black boots. He looked in the bedroom, where earrings and necklaces and chains were scattered over the surface of the dresser they shared, and then in the bathroom, which smelled of her shampoo. Back in the living room, Walter sat in the chair next to the window. In the corner, beside the dining table and the jade plant and the trailing wandering dew, Lacy's finches flitted in their cage. Her books of Goya and Delacroix lay at his feet. And as he looked out through the glass, he could see his car, still running, hot-wired and open to the neighborhood.

It would be best to take the car back to the shopping center and leave it in its place, as if it had been there all along. Then he could walk home and stand watch. He saw for the hundredth time Lacy pulling up to the curb in his car, then stepping out, all in quick motions, coming home again. Just like that. He felt the blood rise in his neck. Lacy was killing him.

EIGHT MONTHS HAD PASSED since Lacy moved in with Walter, but she still kept some things back at home in her parents' big house on St. Mary's Street. If you choose to move in with that man, they'd told her, then don't expect us to support you. You're on your own, her mother said. Her father shrugged. Suit yourself, he said. Be a slut. Shack up with a deaf mechanic.

Lying on her back beside the Eno River, with Tom Daniels nuzzling her shoulder, Lacy thought about going home. She could slip in the back door and run upstairs to her old bedroom unnoticed, maybe gather up some summer clothes from her dresser drawers. She might even take a shower in her own bathroom with the cool white tiles on the floor, the little honeycomb-shaped tiles she used to trace with her bare toes when she was a girl.

At times, she wished she were still a girl, a mere child with her hair drawn up in a ponytail, riding her bike down the sidewalk.

On the ground beneath the big magnolia in the front yard there would be the smell of moss and rainwater, and from the open windows of her house the sound of clattering pots in the kitchen or else Mary, the maid, running the vacuum in the upstairs sitting room. The days would linger into dusk, the fireflies would bob about, her father would come home.

"You know what I'd like to do now?" Lacy said.

Tom lifted his face from her shoulder. "What?"

"To go back to my parent's house and take a bath."

"With me?"

She struggled to sit. "Ha-ha, not exactly," she said. "Get me my shirt."

Tom reached back and took Lacy's shirt, now muddy from the riverbank. Lacy tried to brush the shirt clean. "Now I know I have to go home."

Tom stood and straightened his own clothes. Lacy saw that he had smudged knees, and his shorts were damp at the waistband. She looked away. Suddenly she could not stand the sight of Tom Daniels, so she turned and began to walk along the water's edge, combing her hair with her fingers.

"There's little more wine if you want it," he called.

Lacy said, "Save it for me. I'll drink it on the way back."

She noticed movement in the water downstream; shadows bobbed across the surface until they took the form of two boys walking waist-deep, pushing a raft. Lacy stepped to the water's edge and dipped in a toe. The water was cold. She stepped in to her ankles. "Bring me that bottle!" she shouted, turning to Tom. "I'll drink it here."

Tom was not the type to swim in a cold river, she knew. She felt the urge to step out deeper, to force him to come to her, but the river bottom was rocky, with strands of slime curling in the current. "Here," Tom said, stepping in, "it's too damned cold for me."

Lacy took the bottle without looking at him. The wine satisfied a thirst she didn't know she had; she drank deeply and wished for more. "It's been awhile since I was drunk," she said. Tom stood on the bank behind her, watching. "I wouldn't mind it now."

She stepped in to her thighs.

"I'll get you another bottle if you go all the way in," Tom said.

Lacy turned to face him and smiled. Then she took a breath, lifted her arms, and sank to her knees. Her shirt floated, then settled into the water and clung to her skin. For a brief moment all was still, even the rustling trees along the shore and the boys far downstream, still pushing their little raft, and the birds and the water itself. Tom looked at Lacy, mesmerized, and she looked back and smiled. "Good God, this water's freezing. You owe me some wine."

THE DRIVEWAY BEHIND THE big brick house was empty save for Lacy's black car. Only the rear bumper was visible; the front of the car was hidden within a brick garage at the end of the drive, where ivy crept up the walls and a forest of bamboo leaned high above the roof. Lacy led Tom down the driveway. On either side, bamboo shoots rose from the ground like daggers. "Watch your step," Tom said. Her shorts were still wet against her thighs, and she carried her sandals in one hand. "You could lose a foot if you stepped on one of those."

Lacy wobbled. She was looking for a house key. When she reached her car, she knelt to search the walls of the garage.

Cobwebs lifted at her touch. She patted a flat hand along the gritty ledge. "Got it." She held a single key in her fingers. "My secret key," she said, "my insurance."

Bees hovered over the flowering sweetbush next to the house. Lacy headed toward the back porch, letting her bare feet slough through the grass and plucking clover with her toes. She had drunk most of the second bottle of wine on the way back to town, singing and talking until Tom turned the corner to her street, when she suddenly grew silent. Now Tom stepped behind her and opened the screen door on the porch. "Where do you think your parents are?" he said. Lacy stopped at the lowest step and cast a bitter glance at the sky. "Who knows?" she said. "Sitting at the airport watching the planes fly in."

The tiles on the porch floor were damp and cold, and the couch and the chairs were slumped. All around them was the odor of cold brick and peeling windowsills and ancient, blackened screen. Lacy walked across the porch and turned her key in the back door lock, leading Tom inside. As they walked through a dim hall, a cat appeared in an open doorway and began to follow Lacy, crying. She took the cat in her arms and turned a corner in the kitchen. "Hungry?" she said, and when Tom didn't answer, she said, "Speak up."

He laughed. "I thought you were talking to the cat."

What Lacy noticed at that moment was Tom's white teeth, the way his mouth curved when he smiled, and his faint blond beard. "You funny, sweet guy," she said, going to him. She pressed her body against his, squeezing the cat between them. "Isn't he funny and sweet?" she said in a high voice, talking to the cat. She ran her fingers through the cat's gray fur. "And I do think he has the prettiest blond beard." The cat dropped from her hands to the floor. "One little kiss," she said. Tom leaned in to kiss her mouth, still sweet with wine. But just as he began to pull her to him, she backed away. "You know," she said, smiling, "you could pass for sixteen."

"Then you could pass for twelve," he said.

Lacy turned on her heels. "Nope," she said, "I'm all of twenty-four years old. A self-supporting, tax-paying, sign interpreter for the deaf. A bona fide Florence Nightingale."

Tom leaned against the counter and watched her as she moved unsteadily across the floor.

"What's the appeal?" he said.

"What do you mean, 'what's the appeal?' Deaf people are just like everybody else. They can be smart, or not smart, and they can be really fun or else boring as hell. They can get on your nerves. Or they can tell great jokes. Which hardly anybody ever hears."

"Unless you tell them," Tom said, "unless you interpret for them."

Lacy opened the refrigerator. "Now all I want is food," she said, "but the only thing my parents ever eat is stuff like pickles and cream cheese. Or this date bread."

"But what if you interpret wrong?" Tom went on.

Lacy shrugged. "Nobody knows."

She clanked a knife in a mayonnaise jar, tore ribs of celery from a stalk, took out tuna and black pepper and saltines. "Put on some music."

As he left the kitchen and went out into the open den, Lacy watched him through the butler's window. He'd always been a bit delicate, all the way back when they were in grammar school together and her mother picked him up in the morning in her station wagon. He could never open the car door by himself, since the handle always fooled him and the door swung open so heavily. Lacy watched him pore over her parent's album collection. So now he had a degree in business, just like her father. Had gotten himself a good job back home like her father had, returning home from college to be near his mama.

"OK," she called out from the kitchen. "I'm going upstairs to take a bath."

The hallways in the house were dark, and the carpets tickled her bare feet. She loved the broad floral patterns on the wall on the stairs, and the light that shone from the high window at the landing, and the smooth cold feel of the banister in her palm. She felt all of this even more now that she was nearly drunk, except it was all of one piece—the smell of the carpet with the stiff wool beneath her feet, and then the light, and the banister, and the hovering flowers on the wall.

And then her bedroom, just as she'd left it when she was a teenager going away to college, the four-poster bed in the center, strewn at the posts with strands of plastic beads and faded ribbons from horse shows; the draperies drawn back with a tasseled cord; the dressing table with its white eyelet skirt, and the posters on the walls, Degas and Van Gogh. She sat in the upholstered chair in the corner and leaned back to stare at the ceiling—white, flat, with a long brown crack in the plaster, crooked like a tree limb—and then she stood to peel off her damp shorts and panties and soiled shirt until she was naked. At the mirror above her dressing table she judged herself privately, the way she used to do when she was a girl. She turned sideways, and then more, until she looked over her own shoulder at the image of herself in the mirror—youthful, pale, with skin still cold from the river.

Then she did another thing no one ever saw her do: she spoke to herself in sign. Standing naked at the mirror, she looked at herself as if she were looking at a stranger, and she talked with her hands: *You think you know somebody...you think so but you don't...you think....* It was just words and phrases she acted out in pantomime, but she was exhilarated by them all the same. *You*—she pointed to the mirror—*you think so, but no.*

The afternoon had turned humid, and the air in her room was close. Lacy filled the tub and settled down into the water. It was an old tub, with bird-claw feet and a sloping rim and a stopper on a beaded chain. She shut her eyes. Her tongue was numb with the taste of wine, and her mind was empty save for the sound of the water.

So she didn't notice when Tom stepped into the doorway and looked down at her. The water pounded. Soon it rose beneath her hair, and she felt strands float near her face. There was a faint smell of soap in the room, and she thought of a towel—whether she'd remembered to get one out of the linen closet, whether she'd even remembered to get a mat for the floor. Behind the sound of the running water there came the distant cry of a blue jay, and then the sound of someone moving. A clearing throat, a voice.

"Did you plan to leave me downstairs all day?"

She startled; water sloshed over the sides of the tub. She sat up and covered her breasts with her hands. "Who asked you up here?"

Tom leaned in the doorway and smiled. "You look a lot like that woman in the poster on your wall."

Lacy saw the painted figure, pale as milk, sitting naked on the edge of her tub, washing one of her upturned feet. A dark tendril of hair curled down her bare back.

"Get the hell out."

Tom smiled. "Just like old times."

"What do you mean, old times?" she said. She drew her knees to her chest. "You never came up to my room before."

"No, but you were always throwing me out from somewhere. 'Let's go to the river, Tommy, let's go out in the car.' And then, 'Stop it, Tommy, don't Tommy, I can't.'"

"Oh please," Lacy said, "I didn't ask you up here, and I sure don't plan to take a bath with you watching. So get out."

"You want me to go?"

"That's what I said."

"Really go? Leave you here in the house by yourself? I drove, remember."

Lacy hesitated. She could see her car in the dusty garage. Back in the fall, when she began spending nights with Walter, her parents threatened to take the car away. "Who's making the payments?" her father had said. She saw this as a dare, so she took to going off with Walter in his car, leaving her own car parked in front of her parents' house for days. When she finally packed up one Sunday and moved in with Walter altogether, her parents drove her car deep into the garage and parked it for good.

Tom said, "So? You want me to go? Leave you here?"

Lacy imagined getting in her car and driving it away. She could see her parents coming back, pulling up into the drive, shooting the high beam of their headlights into the garage.

There was a long silence. Lacy looked up at Tom. In the waning afternoon light that shone from the one window in the bath, he was handsome. His face had tanned a little when they were out at the river, and his hair curled against his collar. She drew her knees tighter.

"Just wait for me," she said. "Outside."

Tom disappeared from the doorway, and Lacy sat back. Across the window, the leaves on the trees waved and lifted, and although it was not yet dark, the dappling sunlight fell away. If she'd been alone in the house, she would've gone to lie flat on her bed with her eyes closed, as she often did on a Saturday afternoon when she was a girl. The day would wear on, and she'd lie there with a damp towel across her body, and the sound of birds would enter the room, and the smell of flowers would drift about, and a bee would fly against the screen.

But when she entered her room, Tom was waiting for her. She crossed over to her bed and sat near the wall, turning her back to him. "Looks like you could give me a little privacy," she said.

There was the sound of the rustling mattress. Tom leaned on one arm and crooked a finger over the edge of her towel, pulling it down from her shoulder. "You wouldn't kick me out if I was Walter."

She hadn't thought of Walter for hours, but now she saw him anew, standing before the big window in his house, looking out, and she felt the ache of regret. Walter stood at the window, but she couldn't worry about that now. There was a hand on her skin, the knuckle tracing a line down her shoulder blade, and in the close heat of the afternoon, there was the white sky and the heavy feeling of another failed day, nothing being the way it seemed it would be. The knuckle and then the finger down to the small of her back, and then the feel of the towel dropping down at her bare hips. Walter was watching from the window, and Lacy couldn't help it, she was alone in her old childhood bedroom, with Tom, who made her shiver.

He pushed her against the pillow, and she fell back, exposed to him, and while he straddled her there, smiling and narrowing his eyes at her, a clock ticked somewhere downstairs, and the cat slept in a chair. Across town, Walter waited. And somewhere nearby, her parents drove in their car.

They're out at the airport watching the planes come in, Lacy had said, and she'd imagined it as she spoke it: her mother, with hair colored so many times it was like spun glass, leaning against the car window, and her father at the wheel with his driving gloves on. Their car right at the edge of the runway, the motor idling, with grass growing up around the tires. An absurd picture, something that made her laugh inside. Good old Charlie and Vivian hunkering down low, with planes roaring in for the approach and their ears filling with all that noise.

Or they're at the Merchandise Mart checking out the low prices, she could have said. Or they're playing a rip-roaring round of golf, with Vivian watching from inside the cart, wearing her white cleats, and Charlie hiking up his golf trousers, casting a long look down the fairway to judge the distance—a nine iron, a five?—while the other couple in the foursome, the Dorseys, maybe, or the Buchanans, chuckled about something or other.

She hated thinking about them. Now that she was in her old house, she could feel them everywhere. In the early days, when her mother, the actress, was out late, Lacy puttered around in her bedroom alone while her father played music downstairs and drank. Sometimes he read books. Or else he glued model cars. Lacy's friends came to visit, and they wondered about him. "What's he doing?" a friend would whisper, eyeing him. "Is he playing with toys?"

And then her mother. Lacy could hear her voice: "I'm sorry, but I'm just not able to cope today." She'd say it in the oddest places—while standing in the hallway upstairs with her bath-robe still on and the sun throwing bars of light over the carpet at her feet, or behind the wheel of the car, as Lacy climbed in after a riding lesson. "I'm just a little shaky." When they reached home, her father would be there, busy in the garage with the radio on, and he wouldn't appear ufntil bedtime. By then her mother would be gone, at the theater.

Down the street, there were families. One of them was Tom's, with his little brothers out in the yard and his mother and father in the den, their TV going—the noise of that household!—and behind their house, on the other side of a hedge, the Vernons, with all those children and the thick smell of something frying in the kitchen. Most afternoons, Lacy wandered down the street so she could feel she was part of everything, and she stayed out until it was time for supper and she was sent home.

In the waning light of her room she lay on the bed next to Tom, one arm draped across his damp chest. He ran one hand over her bare shoulders and down her back, and she closed her eyes. Dear Tommy. She saw him in her memory as a skinny boy riding his bicycle in circles in his family's wide, paved drive. Who had he become? Who had she become? The four posters of the bed rose above them like stanchions, looped by plastic beads she'd won at the fair. Outside there was the distant drone of an airplane, and then that same blue jay. She dozed off.

Minutes passed while she lay curled in slumber. The clock ticked. She breathed so silently it was as if she'd disappeared, and her mind was empty. But when Tom moved on the bed, she stirred, and her ears understood the ticking of the clock and the sounds that came through the window. Lacy saw her mother in her dreams, or else she heard a voice, and then there was her father on the stair landing, his heavy steps ascending. She saw his large hand on the banister, but just as suddenly, he faded away. There was the flitting noise of an insect as it flew past the screen. Then Walter appeared—it was his leg next to hers, was it not?—and the sure weight of another body lying next to her in the bed. A feeling of warmth came over her, even in her sleep, and although her mouth was dry, and there was a pain rising behind her ear, she felt deeply content all of a sudden, as if Walter had come to lie beside her in the night.

She reached a toe to feel for him, and when she thought she found his touch, she let her foot rise up the hard shinbone until he responded, toes touching toes—a game she had played in her bed as a little girl. Back then, in the darkness of night, it was the game her father called What's Touching You Now. A big toe, a finger, a thumb, the tip of a tongue. She'd taught the game to Walter once. He heard nothing, felt everything. Tongue, toe, thumb—tiny quiet touches on the neck, the spine. Then another part of the game, the part called Which Feels Best?

A dog was barking down the street, and someone started the engine of a truck. The engine cut off and started again, and the dog barked and barked. Lacy sat up, and there was Tom, naked. She looked at him through the orange light of pain, and she fought back sudden waves of nausea. While the dog kept barking, she cast her mind over the city to wherever her parents might be, riding home, since it was after five o'clock and the heat of the afternoon had dissipated. Supper time. Birds were roosting in trees.

WALTER HAD FINISHED ALL the beer he had. On the TV screen, wrestlers fell against the ropes and then sprang back into the ring. The one with the white hair wore leather wristbands and sandals laced to his knees. Samson. He stood in the center of the ring while his flabby opponent lunged toward him, scissors in hand. To cut his hair, deprive him of his power. The flabby man reached for Samson's hair, grasped a white clump in one fist, and aimed the scissors. Silently, Samson bellowed.

Walter went into the kitchen. There was a little orange juice in the refrigerator. He considered the juice, but reached instead for a bottle of bourbon from the cabinet above. He turned toward the sink. Lacy's coffee cup sat on the counter. With a flick of his hand, he swung the bottle at the cup, feeling in his wrist the collision of glass. The cup rolled on its side. He hit the cup again and watched it shatter.

LACY KEPT HER BACK turned while she dressed. She twisted her hair into a knot. Tom asked her, "Why can't you drive your car anymore?"

"Because," she said, "it really belongs to my parents, and I don't want to have anything to do with them anymore." Her hands shook nervously. "So I'd appreciate it if you'd take me back to Walter's."

She kept her eyes to the floor. She could feel Tom watching her, since she knew she'd made him jealous. But all men were jealous. She looked about the floor. Somewhere, there were her shoes.

"You left them in the car," Tom said.

On the ride across town, he wanted to talk about Walter. What would she tell him? Would she invite him inside the house they shared, and would she introduce him? Lacy pretended to laugh. "Very funny."

"Do you leave him this way often?"

"Only for you, Tom."

"Don't give me that crap. I bet you've cheated on him plenty of times."

Lucy shot him a glance. "What I do is none of your business. But if you want to know the truth, I haven't gone out on Walter once. I haven't cheated on him."

There was silence.

"But you did it for me," he said finally.

The traffic was heavy; they seemed to hit every red light. Lacy reached to turn on the radio, but Tom grabbed her hand and stopped her. "I said, you did it for me."

A bitter taste rose in Lacy's throat. "Let's just drop it," she said.

Tom slapped the steering wheel. "You've always been such a tease," he said. "If you ever noticed that people didn't respond to you, it was because you were always so slippery, so hard to know. One day I'd speak to you, and you'd act like you'd never seen me before, then the next time I'd see you, you'd ask me for a ride. You must've laid plenty of guys, just looking for favors."

Lacy dropped her temple against the window. "Thanks a lot," she said, "you're being really nice."

"I mean, think about it," Tom went on. "What you do now is just perfect. You spend all your time teaching people how to speak in sign language, and you have a deaf boyfriend. Perfect! The two of you have your own language together, but you're still one better. You can hear, and he can't. So you can slip out at night and he won't hear a thing. You can even screw in the next room and he won't know."

Lacy sat upright and gripped the arm of the car door. "You

let me out right here," she said. Tom answered by hitting the accelerator. She tried to roll down the window, but he locked it from his side. Next she tried reaching across him to unlock the windows herself, but he pushed her away. The car rocked from side to side. All the way down Peace Street they struggled, Lacy jabbing with her elbow, Tom holding her arm. "I'm walking!" she shouted, but Tom only laughed. Up ahead, another light was about to turn red. As they rolled to a stop, she opened the door to the curb and leapt out, stopping to look back at Tom, who was trapped behind the wheel. She knew people were watching from the cars behind them; she knew how this must look. The door hung open, cars idled at the light. When the light changed, she kicked the door shut with one bare heel.

SOMETIME DURING THE AFTERNOON, Buck found a tattered old cap, which he now held between his paws as he lay on the grass. As long as Walter sat on the front steps, the little dog was content to chew the cap, ripping at the bill until the fabric pulled away in shreds. Whenever Walter shifted his spot, Buck dropped the cap and stood, ready to follow. But Walter was still. He kept his eyes fixed on the end of the street, where he could watch approaching cars, sipping bourbon. He drew back between the shrubs by his door and watched from the shadows. Two women strolled past, and they reminded him of his sisters, the way their big horse hips swung lazily from side to side. Good old Mary Jane and Elaine, they were already ancient before he was born. Held his burred head tight and shouted in his face, their puffy red lips making wide O's and E's. He was their little pet, stone deaf. For his sake, they learned to finger-spell, and they spelled

out every damned letter. W–A–L–T–E–R! S–U–P–P–E–R I–S O–N
T–H–E T–A–B–L–E!

The memory filled him with emotion, so much so that he had
to turn away from the street to do something with his hands. He
began plucking weeds, feeling cool dirt beneath his nails. *Lacy,
Lacy, Lacy.* While he worked, he thought of her name, how different it was, how lovely and wicked. She moved like a dancer, with
slender legs. He pictured her tending to her finches. She'd open the
little door and offer her hand, and the birds would tilt their heads
just so, and one would step a clawed foot onto her palm. She'd talk
to the bird, and it would turn a black eye in her direction.

Walter tugged at the weeds, and the idea came to him that the
birds would like to be outside in the fresh air. He went in to get
them, lifting the cage from its hook, and carried them out to the
front walk. They flew wildly against the side of the cage, and
feathers floated. At the top of the cage, a little bell swung from
side to side. But in the bright daylight, the cage suddenly looked
dingy, and the birds looked tiny and trapped. Buck sniffed at the
cage, and the birds flapped from one side of the cage to the other.
How pathetic they were.

Down in the weeds, he discovered an earthworm writhing on
the ground. He took it between two fingers, carried it over to
the birdcage and dropped it between the bars. Then he opened
the cage door and set them free.

TWO BLOCKS AWAY, UP near the Methodist church, Lacy was walking barefooted on the sidewalk. She'd left her shoes with Tom,
and she'd forgotten about Walter's car until just this moment.
How could she have been so stupid, she wondered, forgetting

everything—her clothes, her shoes, and worst of all, the car, with Buck trapped inside? For she'd finally remembered Buck, and now he was all she could see. Panting, scratching at the windows for air. He would become so parched from thirst, he'd scratch the upholstery and windows. And—Lacy dared not let herself picture it—he could die in the heat.

She walked with the rush of traffic at her side, slapping at her pockets, feeling for keys. Her mind went over the day: the ride with Tom, the river, the market where they bought the wine, her house. There was the bath upstairs. Her clothes all over the floor. And the keys, the keys. Treading carefully on the gritty sidewalk, she wished for keys. How silly she must look, teetering along in her little shorts, her hair tangled loose in a knot, barefooted. She felt herself grow small. The great limbs of old oaks hung over the sidewalk, and she passed beneath them. Soon it would be her birthday. The warm air, and the birdsong, and the sweet fragrance of wisteria on the vine: all of it formed a continuous memory of her childhood, birthday after birthday, spring after spring. She was still a child, wasn't she? Mischievous and fun. So wouldn't Walter forgive this?

HE'D FOUND A RAKE, and with Buck at his side, he gathered leaves in a pile by the front walk. Across the street, a light came on in the window looking out onto the porch, and a shadow passed by. Down the street, someone lit charcoal. Walter swallowed; he'd hardly eaten all day. If Lacy were home, he'd suggest a barbecue, and they'd drive to the store for steaks. She'd play her music in the car, and once they got home, she'd turn on the stereo. Even though the music was lost to him, Walter would be happy to see her sway in the kitchen. He might go to the stereo and turn up the volume as far as it would go, and the music would shake the floor in pulses he could feel in his spine.

He raked patterns in the ground. He could see the daylight change before his eyes, a sad shifting, and his stomach grew tight. *If night fell, and no sign of her.* He gripped the rake and looked down at the birdcage, empty now. The chill of evening settled in, and from far off there was the scent of something flowery, and then the scent of a barbecue grill. A different light came on across the street, a soft and homey light. And at last, like a scene from a movie, there was at the end of the street a thin white figure on the sidewalk, approaching on uncertain legs. The white shirt nearly glowed in the half-light. Walter watched, peering across the distance. Lacy. He leaned against the rake. There was the leftover taste of bourbon on his tongue.

He saw her pale, bare legs, the way she looked naked in her bare feet. She took delicate, careful steps as if she were trying to make herself scarcely visible, as if she could creep into view. Buck lifted his head and perked up his ears, and when he spied Lacy coming, he leapt to greet her. He ran down the sidewalk in a flash of white.

Walter watched her take Buck into her arms, saw Buck kicking his back legs against her waist and licking her ear. Walter couldn't help but feel relieved to see her again. But he hated to see how easily she hugged the dog. Hadn't she left him in the car for hours? And how did she think he got back home so that he could jump in her arms now?

She set Buck down on the sidewalk, and seeing Walter, she waved. But he held his ground. She reached back and took down her hair, shaking it loose. The closer she came, the more tousled she appeared. Walter took it as a sign. He remembered her jeans in the back of his car, her things strewn on the floor of the back seat. She had been up to something. His heart began to race, and he had to work to breathe.

"The car," Walter signed. "Where?"

She lowered her head. Even though she was still some distance away, Walter could see the shift in her eyes. "The car?" he said.

"I will explain," she signed back. And again, "I will tell you." She picked up her pace, tripping barefooted along the sidewalk. "The keys," she said. "I lost the keys, so I had to walk home." Buck nipped at her ankles. "But Buck—how did he get here? Did he come home, or did you find him?"

Walter examined her face, ignoring her signing hands. Her cheeks were flushed; everything about her looked sweaty and damp. With her hands she said, "Walter, I'm so sorry," and he listened vaguely in his way. She was lying.

"Lacy," he said with his mouth. Speech rose from his throat. "Lacy, you…." The words tumbled forth, angry, gurgling, and as he spoke, he found new strength in his voice. Even Buck looked at him, lifting his ears.

Along the street, some windows were open in the houses. So it was possible that anyone could hear, in a quiet moment, the distant sound of traffic up on Peace Street, or the stray sound of a car passing along Vass Avenue. And mixed in those sounds, like the sudden caw of a crow, the low and muffled sound of Walter Virgili's voice as he spoke loudly to Lacy. "Say! Where have you been?"

He stepped from his place on the lawn, and the rake dropped silently to the ground. He took her by both arms, squeezing the soft muscles at her shoulders, and drew her hands up to his face. "Were—you—gone—allnight?"

She leaned against him and pushed her way up the hill toward the house. "Just let me explain," she cried, and the sound of her voice carried in the air. But Walter avoided reading her lips; instead he watched her eyes. She pushed him up the hill, and he let her push, walking backwards, still holding her arms. Her drawn-up fists lay against his chest as the two struggled onto the grass, and the smell of crushed wild onions rose beneath their feet.

For a moment, it was as if they were dancing. With one quick motion, Walter let go of Lacy's wrists and took both her hands into one of his big hands, squeezing, and then with his other hand at her back, he pulled her closer until she could smell the bourbon on his lips and he could see the tell-tale rosy bruise on her neck, just below one ear. "Why do you do this to me?" he said at last, the words running together. Tears gathered in her eyes. "I didn't mean to," she said, and as she said it, she yearned to pull herself free and speak with her hands. But Walter would not let her go. "You just don't know what this does to me, Lacy…," he began. He moaned her name, twice. And then, because he couldn't help himself, he lowered his mouth to hers and kissed her.

He lifted Lacy into him, and she rose on her toes. There was somewhere the smell of wine—was it merely the taste on her tongue?—and then there was the dampness at her waist, which he could feel with his one free hand as he pulled her tightly against his body. He tested the waistband with his fingers, and she squirmed at his touch. And then the villainous pink bruise. As if to take it away, he lifted his hand and placed it against the base of her neck. He kissed the spot. "Don't speak," he said, and she nearly dropped to her knees. He pulled her along the front walk to the house, passing the birdcage, empty in the coming dusk. Lacy didn't notice that the birds were missing, an over-sight for which he was suddenly grateful. He pulled her up the steps to the door and shoved her inside.

AT TIMES LIKE THESE, when Lacy knew she had upset Walter, she loved him most. Anger changed him utterly, until in her eyes he became no longer the one who couldn't hear, the one who couldn't answer the phone or talk to the mailman on the street. When he was angry, he became the only kind of man she ever wanted, and she thrilled at the sound of his gruff voice as he talked out loud. He slammed drawers, ran his flat hand across a table and let things fly, bringing to life their mute, still home.

Now, as he moved about the house, Walter walked heavily, leading her by the hand. She could feel the blood in his fingers. He led her into the living room and switched on a light beside the couch. He forced her to sit. "See if you can make me believe you."

She looked up at him. "It was so beautiful this morning," she began, "and I couldn't sleep any longer. And the air was already hot, and I was thinking about summer. And you were sleeping, and I just couldn't, so I got up and thought I would go out for some breakfast...."

"And take Buck," Walter said.

"Yes, and Buck followed so I let him get in the car and he came. But then up at Rhew's Grill I saw some friends from the old days and they said they wanted to go out to the river and that they would drive, and then you know how things go...."

"The way things go?" Walter said with his hands, and Lacy answered him, "The way things go, one thing leads to another."

Lacy continued, creating a story from other stories in her past, how she had met two of her old girlfriends, how it had been so long since she'd seen them, it was like a reunion. So she went with them to the river, and yes she forgot all about poor Buck and then when she remembered, she was so worried, but at least thank goodness! You found him in time.

And the car, she was going to say, but she hesitated.

She knew Walter was watching her mouth even while she spoke with her hands. It was a look of fascination—of adoration, even—and although sometimes he made her feel uncomfortable, she loved to think she could possess him, that simply by talking, and by letting him watch her this way, she could become irresistible to him. She stopped and folded her arms; she fixed her gaze into the space between her knees. And then, just as she expected he would, Walter leaned over and turned off the light. He took her in his arms and held her close to his chest, warming her chilled bare thighs with his hands and tickling her neck with his breath.

A shadow interrupted their embrace—across the front door, blocking the last square of daylight in the room. And then the gritty sound of shoes on the stoop outside, a sound that only Lacy could hear. She stiffened. Lifting her head to peer over Walter's shoulders, she spotted Tom. He leaned into the screen door and pressed his face close. When he knocked on the door, Walter sat up abruptly as if he could hear the sound, and Tom's shadow danced. Walter turned to face the door, but just as quickly, Lacy jumped up and crossed the room.

For a moment, Walter stayed on the couch watching Lacy. She was straightening her shorts and tugging at the hem of her blouse, pulling it down over her waist. Her hands ran over her thighs, smoothing, smoothing, while this guy (Walter recognized him—his lean physique, his boy's haircut, someone Lacy knew) stood on the other side of the screen. He was talking, Lacy was talking, and as Walter watched them he could tell that things were turning complicated, the way Lacy shrugged her shoulders, the way he placed a hand on the door frame and leaned into it, talking, and the way he kept shifting his stance. He reached into his pocket and pulled out keys.

Seeing the keys, Walter leapt to his feet and pulled Lacy away from the door. Slapping the screen with the heel of his hand, he knocked Tom backwards. "Give them," he said. He threw the door open and clawed the keys out of Tom's hand. "Fucking bastard," he said, "those my keys."

What filled Walter's mind then, what kept him from chasing Tom to his car and punching him, was the memory of the rosy bruise behind Lacy's ear. He could just see the treachery now: Lacy's lifting mouth, this guy's long kiss, and later, the soft pink flame he left on her neck. Walter closed his fingers over the keys as he watched Tom hurry to his car and get in. The little light in the car shone briefly over his golden head, and then the light blinked off and the car drove away.

Walter licked his lips and swallowed. Suddenly he felt as if something was caught in his throat, he was so thirsty. The soft light of the street lamps washed over the sidewalk, and the bars of the birdcage gleamed. He cleared his throat. He stepped back into the house and found Lacy in the middle of the room, limp, a mere shadow against the one light that shone from the kitchen in the back. He walked past her, brushing her arm roughly. "A drink," he said. "A drink, Lacy, and then it's you and me."

There was some bourbon left in the bottle, so Walter took a long swallow, leaving enough for Lacy. He stepped back into the living room with the bottle in his hand. "Drink up." He dangled the keys. Instinctively, he knew they would ring. He lifted the keys and let them wave before Lucy's eyes, and then he tilted the bottle to her mouth. A drop of bourbon trickled down her chin.

A pause—and Walter threw the bottle against the wall. Buck raced into the room and began jumping at Lacy's legs, excited by the noise, but she kicked him away with her bare toes. He thought she was playing with him. He leapt backwards, then charged, gnawing at her feet.

She caught her breath. She looked up at Walter. "At least Buck forgives me," she said plainly. He stared into her eyes, ignoring her speaking mouth. "You know what I said," she went on. "Buck forgives me. You should, too."

Walter tossed the keys onto the couch and lifted his hands to sign. "But Buck cannot see the kiss mark on your neck."

Lacy touched her fingers to the spot, and Walter grabbed her hands. "Do you think I will kiss where he kissed," he said with his voice, "I kiss there?"

When she didn't respond, he pulled her over to the stereo, where he put the needle down on a record and turned the volume as high as it would go. The thin walls of the little house shook, and Walter felt the throb of music in his knees. As if the music had the power to bring all his other senses to life, he could sense the screen door shaking to the rhythm and he could see Lacy's birds hovering in the dark. Suddenly he could feel many things—the bristled white hair on Buck's hard back as he pranced about, and the bouncing shadow of a moth as it flew against the ceiling beneath the kitchen light, and the bottle shining on the floor against the baseboard. Lacy's wrists pulsed beneath his fingers, and her eyelids fluttered behind a strand of hair that had fallen over her eyes.

He began to dance. With heavy steps, he pushed Lacy in front of him in a clumsy waltz, all the while tracing a forefinger over the hickey on her neck. "Dance with me, Lacy," he said, "feel the music with me." His fingers dug into her wrists. He moved a finger beneath her chin, lifting it to expose her neck. He leaned in, pressing his nose to her throat, nuzzling, and then he touched her neck with his tongue. "Who's touching you now?" he said, and then he drew back to look into her eyes. "His tongue, or Walter's tongue?"

A tiny red light blinked in the corner of the room—the telephone. Walter saw it first, cocking his head, and then Lacy saw it, too. Again and again the light blinked simultaneous with the ring. Walter looked at the light, then back to Lacy. He grinned. "Call for you," he said. "So answer it."

He kept his eyes fixed on her as she crossed the room. She seemed to teeter drunkenly, her shorts tight between her thighs. For the first time, he noticed that the back of her blouse was muddy. She picked up the phone. He could see her say hello and then listen calmly. When she spoke at last, and he saw her face brighten, Walter felt the pull of an invisible curtain, the same curtain that was drawn wherever he went, where people spoke but he heard nothing. They were in their world, and he was not. They lay in the darkness speaking. They spoke over the distance of a single wire. They sang, and people clapped for them. They talked with their backs turned, and they heard words floating in air.

Lacy held the phone and listened. Then her tongue touched a place within the center of her mouth—the letter T. Her lips opened slightly, then softly closed—OM. Walter was sure he'd understood it. The pain of recognition was so stunning, he felt the room spin. He seized the lamp next to the couch, jerked its cord from the socket, and let it fly. Lacy jumped, dropping the phone, and ran to the kitchen. Walter followed and caught her by the hair. He thought he heard her scream. She fell to the floor, but he wouldn't let her stay there. He pulled her to her feet and gripped her by the neck, feeling the blood in her veins rise warmly within his fingers. When she broke loose, he watched her run.

The music blared on, but he couldn't hear it, nor could he know that Buck had fled from the house altogether and was now running, nose to the sidewalk, up Vass Avenue and out of sight.

THE APRIL AIR WAS cold, the sun having gone down hours ago, and there was the smell of smoke. Someone was burning wood in a barbecue grill, or perhaps the college students on Peace Street had started a bonfire. Doors closed, and the sound carried through the neighborhood. Someone stepped on their porch and called a dog. There was a distant siren. A car's roaring engine.

A young woman rushed across the street and banged on a door. She banged again, and then she cried out. If anyone heard her then, they would say it was a frightening thing, the way her small voice cried. She banged on the diamond-shaped window of the door, her white blouse turning yellow in the lemon light of a mosquito bulb.

She was barefooted and bare-legged. She held her knees together and stepped from one foot to the other. She knocked again, and she let out another cry. At last the door opened for her, and the low voice of an older woman entered the night air. The girl stepped quickly inside, as if ducking in. And then the door shut.

It was warm in the room where they sat at a table, the girl still shaking nervously, wringing her hands. "Oh," she said, "I thought he would kill me, the way he came after me. I had to get out of there. I went to the bathroom, he's deaf you know, and I opened the window and climbed out. He's still in there. He's probably looking for me."

Then: "Do you have a cigarette?"

The woman turned to go to the kitchen, and the girl bent double at the knees. "He's going to be looking for me," she said.

In her mind she could see a dark scene. One light in Walter's kitchen—that one pillbox light—and Walter wandering from room to room, passing the kitchen again and again, calling her name.

The woman came back with a pack of cigarettes and a lighter. The girl took a cigarette from the pack. "He's going to be looking for me," she said again.

The woman didn't say anything, although she knew who they were: the pretty girl and that deaf fellow. She'd watched him in his yard, and she'd heard his strange way of talking. The girl— she had a way of coming and going all the time, a way of driving off, very fast, up the street. Now as she looked closely at her face, she detected purple shadows beneath her eyes, as if she'd been without sleep for a while. Her hair was a mess. And her clothes—she was barely dressed. She put her cigarette between dry lips and let it dangle loosely while she talked. The cigarette rose and fell with each word. Finally she lifted the lighter and flicked it. Her face glowed briefly in the flame. A beautiful young lady, the woman thought: truly beautiful. She watched her draw deeply, take the cigarette down between two fingers, exhale. She looked out into the room, drew in more smoke, then exhaled loudly. "I just don't know…," she began.

"Did you hear how he played the stereo so loud? Did you hear how he screamed?" She rose from her chair and went to the window that faced the street. From this view, Walter's house was barely visible, there were so many tree branches. The branches swayed slightly, and the pale light of the street lamp glimmered in the leaves. "If you opened your window now, you'd hear him," she said. She stood solemnly watching from the window, smoking. "You know he's deaf. Did I say that already?"

In the silence that followed, they could just barely hear music across the street. The girl took one last deep draw of smoke into her lungs and dropped her hand by her side. She rose on her toes and pressed her face close to the windowpane. "I think I see him," she said. Her voice was suddenly breathy, and there was new light in her eyes.

She turned to the table and crushed out the cigarette. She smiled. "Well, thank you," she said, "I think I better go back now." She ran her hands over her hips and tugged at her blouse. Then she went to the door and let herself out.

The woman listened for the girl's steps on the porch as she left, and then she went to the window to watch her cross the street. She had a sudden urge to lift the window, just a crack, so she could listen for the cries of the deaf man as he saw his girlfriend return. Sometimes there was great noise that came from that house. But mostly it was quiet.

FOODS OF THE BIBLE

n Sunday School we learned about the wheat and the chaff. Okay, so everybody has their weird memories. Our teacher lined us up. Wheat on the right, chaff on the left. Some of you are good, some of you are bad. Some will rise to heaven, others will descend to hell. She pretended to carry in a load of wheat. I'm carrying in wheat from the harvest, she said, and slapped it invisibly to the floor, God the harvester. Next she grabbed a broom and started smashing. Oh, the violence! She spread her legs and planted her feet firmly on the hooked rug. Whacked the make-believe wheat, talking all along. The wheat has to be thrashed, she said, just like we ourselves must be thrashed from time to time. Shiny pearls of sweat formed on her powdered forehead. Because, she went on, nearly out of breath, if all we do is go our merry way, we get the idea that life is easy street! She gave the floor several final good whacks. But listen, darlings, no one's free from toil and trouble.

One of the girls fought back tears. She was chaff. Even though I was wheat, I could sympathize.

So why were we divided in two, a kid asked. He, too, was chaff. He was also the same kid who, when we learned about Noah's Ark, wondered what kept the pairs of bees from flying off. Was this now easy street on the right and toil and trouble on the left? Were some of us going to be rich and some of us poor? Whatever happened to the good and the bad and the wheat and the chaff? And what was chaff, anyway?

The wheat is what remains after it gets thrashed, our teacher said. You make bread out of it. The chaff is the stuff you throw away, like carrot peels.

Sadly, she said, we can't all be wheat.

The next Sunday she brought in corn. A reinforcing lesson, she said. Again we were divided up—not wheat/chaff this time but corn/cornmeal. She set a hard ear of corn on the table and began pounding it with the bottom of her shoe. Pretend the corn is wheat, she said. Kernels flew like gravel, everybody shielded their eyes. Next she poured various grinds of corn into bowls: hominy, grits, cornmeal. See, she said, the harder you're cracked, the finer you become.

At once, complicating subgroups arose. What, the smart kid asked, is good and bad now? Shouldn't we be divided into four groups? Corn, hominy, grits, cornmeal. The good, the not as good, the bad, and the worst?

Well, said a girl, also known to be very smart, it all depends on what you're serving for supper.

Here our teacher got really flustered. Please, babies, she cried, this isn't a cooking lesson, this is life! She slapped down her shoe, sending up a cloud of corn dust. And then, to our gleeful horror, she choked.

MATING DAY

G o just beyond that clump of brambles, and you'll be on railroad tracks. Train goes through here all day carrying coal. Poke around to see what you can find. It's real rubbly copper-colored dirt by the tracks, just like it is here. But poke around, and I guarantee you there will be bones of puppies. Let it rain, and they'll lift up in the dirt so you can spot them when you're walking, little white rib bones and spines. The longer they're out there, the more they get crumbled and buried in the dust, filtering into the ground like seed. Bones of puppies I could have saved, ought to have saved, ought still to save. But I am not God, and what goes on below me here in this house I cannot control.

Like the sunrise—I can't control that—or the rain, or whether a bitch will go in heat in June or July. From where I sit, I'm about to come to the conclusion that you can't control much of what goes on in life. Certainly not the train. Certainly not a dog. And definitely not human beings. I've got two little boys and two teenage daughters living here in this house and they all have a mind of their own. And I've got Jim, who gets a fix on something and won't let it go. For the past few years, it's been puppies, which he loves to bring into this world and then carry on out of this world, lost in the woods, or vanished up on the mountain hunting in the night, or off into town to be sold to anyone who's just stupid enough to pay for the make-believe papers Jim's written up on those dogs. AKC registered. Kennel club approved. Nine litters in all. So far.

Now tell me that ain't an addiction. Nine litters of pups in the past two years, all types, running around under this house in the dust, rolling in the yard, chewing the porch steps till they're round as broom handles. And cute as all get-out. But soon as they get old enough, they run down the hill and get up in those brambles and get hit by the train. The children come running, tears rolling down their faces, crying that the puppies have been killed.

You could predict it. With a train nearby, running through at sixty-five miles an hour. I've had my own nightmares about seeing a child get run over by that train. I've thought about it so much that it's like it's already happened, the whole scene. And the thing that gets me most is when I think about the train hitting one of my little boys and we can't find him, can't find where his body landed after the impact. If you don't know what I mean, then you haven't seen something big get hit by a train, like a cow. A cow gets hit, and the train knocks it clear into the air. For a few seconds it looks like the train carries it down the tracks, lifting it like a flag—a heavy white cow, legs kicking to one side in slow motion. Cow disappears into the woods on the other side. Sounds like a limb has fallen out of a tree.

You might think I'd be used to all this life-and-death, these animals being born around my house, and these kids running in, growing up, and Jim bringing home more dogs to feed. You might think I'd be callous, but I'm not. Every life is important to me, even puppies. So if you want to know the truth I'm tired of watching Jim mate his dogs, because it's just more life wasted. People aren't all coming out here to this never-never land to get themselves a new pup. People aren't just standing in line. So what happens to all those pups? They wander and get lost, probably some of them starve in the woods. And then there's the train, knocking those little pups off the tracks as if they were just pennies on the rails.

But it's a mating day. You can either stay here in this little room with me or you can go on out back, it's your choice. Whenever there's mating, I choose to stay within. The girls, too, because Jim don't believe in letting a girl watch two coupling dogs. He would rather protect them from a sight like that. Maybe he feels sorry for the bitch—maybe he hates to think of his girls winding up like her, trapped in a small space with a male so full of passion it's like anger—or maybe he's just afraid of the wages of sin. Maybe, since he's the one who invites the male dog into the pen (wide eyes and open nostrils, ears tight against the side of its face), just maybe since he's the one who lets the male dog in on his own female dog, he starts to feel bad for her—feels it as if it's happening to *himself.* Maybe that's why he won't allow his girls to be there, too. Like he's been given the heart of a girl for a brief spell and feels so sorry he just can't have his own daughters there to witness.

So I sit in here, and the girls watch television over there in the TV room, and here come the dogs. Each time Jim invites someone new up here to let their dog get a chance with Princess, or with his precious Sadie of Blackstone, they'll come walking through this living room as if it's the only way to get to the back pen, which it isn't, but Jim is too lazy and too preoccupied to tell them otherwise. I watch them come through and just wait to see if they've got manners enough to speak. Most do. One man even brought over a whole ham to pay for letting his dog go up to stud. That man was so happy for his Labrador retriever you would've thought he was bringing in his own son, parading that sleek dog through here like he was escorting him to Hollywood. And you know what? It didn't take. Princess spent close to an hour skirting out from under that black lab, and then when they finally mated it was real short, no more than one or two minutes, and then it was done. Never got a single puppy.

But most dogs know what to do. Sometimes there will come such noise from the back pen that you just have to go and see if puppies haven't been created right out of thin air. Usually it's a hungry male, first time, and he goes jumping on whatever bitch is the one in heat and then jumps on the other one, too, just in case, and can't get started, and the boys try to help by getting in the middle and trying to hold on so the male can mount steady and then they'll all spill over and squeal. It is truly all just so carnal that sometimes, when I pull up here in this corner in my wing-back chair, it helps if I spend time with the Bible, which I'm about to do. Stay if you like, but I'm about to read the Scriptures.

And Jacob said unto them, My brethren, whence be ye? And they said, Of Haram are we. And he said unto them, Know ye Laban the son of Nabor? And they said, we know him. And

he said unto them, Is he well? And they said, He is well: and,
behold, Rachel his daughter cometh with the sheep.

Now, when Rachel cometh with the sheep, I like to imagine her
with swinging skirts and rings on her toes. She comes walking
out with her curly-horned sheep turning up dust under their
little cloven hooves. They are beautiful gray wooly sheep, and
they follow her as if she is the shepherd queen. She is so beautiful
in the midst of her sheep that Jacob gets tears in his eyes. It's
one of the most romantic passages in the Bible.

And it came to pass, when Jacob saw Rachel the daughter
of Laban his mother's brother, and the sheep of Laban his
mother's brother, that Jacob went near and rolled the stone
from the well's mouth, and watered the flock of Laban his
mother's brother. And Jacob kissed Rachel, and lifted up his
voice, and wept.

Jacob had got word that if he would go to Laban's house, he
would meet his future wife. So when he sees Rachel with those
sheep, parading through, coming toward the well, as pretty as
she is, and he learns that she is the daughter of Laban, he is
overcome. It is how I would have felt if I had been told to go to
Bertie County, which is where Jim grew up, to the home of his
father Daniel (Daniel Milton), and there I'd find my husband.
Or I could be told to visit Milton's Ceramics & Curios and there
would be—you guessed it—Jim. And Jim would be out back
mixing concrete, sleeves rolled up to his shoulders, and I would
know he was the one. And I would weep.

Or he could come find me, in the house of my father, the Rev.

Robert Hemley, and I would be sweeping the front porch, and he would look up from the sidewalk and see me there and weep. Which is almost the way it actually happened. It was midday, hot as it gets, and I took the broom outside to get some air. I swished the broom and watched the street, looking for someone to wave to, like Jim, who rode past my house everyday like clockwork carrying bags of sand and whatnot. On that day, hot as it was, he decided to stop. Pulled up to the curb, got out, stepped forward, and asked for a drink. "I'm just about to die in this heat," he said, and then he looked up at me on the porch and said, "aren't you?" as if we had been having a long conversation and he had just made this observation about the weather.

Queerest thing. I never would've expected it in a million years, but it made me so happy to have him approach. I said something like, "Well, yes, it's got to be the hottest day on record." I stepped inside and got him a glass of cool water, and when I stepped back out he was already on the porch leaning against the post. A little trickle of sweat ran into his red sideburns. His face was kind of gritty, but I thought it was the most beautiful boy's face I'd seen. Like they say in the Bible, I could've wept.

But look at how things turn out. We've been married for eighteen years, ten of them in this same house on the hill by the tracks, and we've got two little boys tall as I am and two girls about to blossom, sure enough. Boyfriends drive past in the middle of the night. You can hear their cars roll down the hill, engines rumbling. Sometimes you hear voices coming from the car windows, but you can't make out what they're saying. I can only imagine. ("Reckon Cindy's already sleeping? Reckon she'll come out if we sit here long enough?")

I would love to warn them with a pistol, but then I think about

Jim up on my porch. If my mother had come after him that day, if she had come outside and asked him just what did he mean by stopping his truck and asking for a drink of water, then I would have been so embarrassed I might've left home.

But I'm not sure people even get embarrassed anymore about anything. *Anything.* Take the dogs. Whole families will come waltzing through here with their male at stud. I swear sometimes they look as hungry as the dog, all smiles as if they're about to watch an X-rated movie. On the one hand I think they're right—it's sex they're about to witness. On the other hand, it's just dogs mating, for Christ sake. You don't have to go far to see something like that. You want to watch mating, you can watch it. You can see birds do it in flight in the spring. You can see squirrels. See cows in the field. Truthfully, if you want a show, watch *horses.* But people come in my house, walking through with their big old mutt who's already got the scent of a bitch filling his whole brain, whites of his eyes showing, and he puts his nose to the floor and starts tugging on the leash. "Whoa," they say, "not yet, not yet."

Lord, if I didn't keep my eyes on this Bible, I'd go crazy.

> *And Laban had two daughters: the name of the elder was Leah, and the name of the younger was Rachel. Leah was tender-eyed; but Rachel was beautiful and well-favoured. And Jacob loved Rachel; and said, I will serve thee seven years for Rachel, thy younger daughter.*

What I want to know is, what is tender-eyed? Are tender eyes soft and brown and slow to blink? Does a woman with tender eyes respond with kindness, giving a tender look? Or does it mean she wears glasses? Here you have Leah and Rachel, sisters, and one is tender-eyed and the other is beautiful. One is gorgeous and the other is so near-sighted that her eyes are in a perpetual squint. One is older and one is younger. One is out by the well when Jacob comes, walking with her sheep, and the other is trapped indoors. One is absolutely so wonderful that Jacob goes right up to her and gives her a kiss and weeps. The other is, who knows? Elbow-deep in bread dough.

Jacob wants Rachel so much he becomes a servant for seven years. Imagine him out in the fields tending to livestock every day and then coming in at night and sitting around the family table looking across at Rachel, his beloved. This goes on for seven years. But when the time comes for Jacob to actually marry Rachel, Laban gives him Leah! And Jacob is so stupid, he doesn't even notice. He climbs in her tent and kisses her mouth, makes love to her all night, and thinks it's Rachel.

Just put yourself in Leah's shoes, though. Think about her being set up in the tent of matrimony, perfume in her hair, fresh from a bath. Think of the way she feels when Jacob first embraces her and bares his chest, groaning the name of her sister in the darkness, "Rachel, oh Rachel." Does it not make you feel a little bitter? Don't you just feel sorry for poor Leah? She could be us! Because here we are, us women, all inside this house, you and me and the girls biding our time as if nothing is happening here this afternoon, when outside there are men hustling around the dog pen lining up the stud and the bitch, and the boys are giggling and getting their little hands right in the middle, and their daddy is allowing that—no, he's *encouraging* that, because he believes animal husbandry is a natural science for men and boys. And here we sit, the girls with a game show on and you and me in this little living room (turn on a light if you like, I know it's dark) waiting for the act to be completed so we can go on with something else for the rest of the day.

It's like Jacob himself is out there in the dog pen, making arrangements, full of blind passion. And the dogs are willing because they're dumb as posts. And because they have no other choice.

And Laban said, It must not be done in our country, to give the younger before the first-born.

STILL YOU'VE GOT TO hand it to Laban, he was definitely on the side of his ugly firstborn daughter. Gave her a handmaiden named Zilpah and slipped her in with Jacob over what was bound to be the loudest fight between two sisters you ever heard. Rachel screams and cries that Jacob kissed her first, loved her most, and followed her around like a puppy dog, so why on earth would her father turn around and give him Leah? This, she says, is not fair!

But Jacob does get Rachel after all. What he does is, he bides his time. He's already been given Leah, who brought along her handmaiden Zilpah (a bonus), and then after seven more years (by now he's been living in Laban's house for fourteen years— Rachel is not getting any younger), Laban lets him have Rachel too. Also Rachel's handmaiden, Bilhah. That's four women total.

Which is a more efficient way to populate the world than the way we do it now. When it takes nine months to get one baby, you've got to have a lot of women to create the twelve tribes of Israel. This is how God plans it out: because he feels sorry for Leah, whose father has sneaked her under the wire and whose husband doesn't want her, God lets her have babies. Leah delivers Reuben, and Simeon, and Levi, and Judah. But Rachel can't have any babies. She's barren as a garden in winter, which is God's way of evening everything out: Rachel has her beauty, she has her flock of sheep, she has her adoring Jacob. So she can't have everything. She can't have babies too. But she goes to Jacob anyway and says, Give me children, or else I die.

It can't happen, she knows, but as long as her handmaiden, Bilhah, has Jacob's baby, she's fine with it. In her eyes, Bilhah is the same thing as her! When Jacob goes into the bedroom with Bilhah, Rachel is all for it! And when Bilhah starts having babies, Rachel is ecstatic! She thinks they're hers!

I'm sorry, but this is too much for me to believe. There's not a woman I know who would look at her husband's baby boy—that baby having been conceived and delivered by another woman out in the open so all can know—and be happy. It's as if I watched Jim march over to visit Mrs. Monroe, our nearest neighbor on Yellow Sulphur Rd., whereupon she would conceive his baby and then carry that baby for nine months and bear that baby, and I would be so happy that I'd march on down with a baby gift and say welcome!

Forgive me, but that's dog behavior. Only dogs will share a male with gladness, carry puppies in their bellies and go hunting with nipples dragging the forest floor, and then nurse another litter if one should come along. Only dogs will get so confused as to which pup belongs to which mama.

In the Bible, Leah has four babies, then Rachel's servant has two, then Leah gets jealous to see Rachel rocking baby boys so she has to have more for herself. But by this time Leah's also barren so she brings in her handmaiden Zilpah, and Zilpah has one. Now listen to what Leah says when she sees that Zilpah is about to deliver that baby: A troop cometh. I like to imagine poor Zilpah laying up in labor, eyes squeezed shut in pain, with Leah at her side saying "a troop cometh!" At which point Leah goes into utter shock.

When I read that, I have sympathy for all things female. Sometimes, I can actually sense the whole female species of the world, the female animals groaning in labor, and the female fishes swimming and releasing their eggs into the water like foam, watching for the male fishes to come and spray their sperm. They swim around and the babies hatch and then they have to watch in fear for the male fishes to come back and actually eat the babies, like so many male species do—devour the young. I think about the bird that returns to her nest to find her eggs have been shattered. Does she pick up the pieces and place them gently in a corner of the nest, loving them still, or does she fly away and forget? I can even feel sympathy for female plants, stretching their flowers to the sun, their ovaries drinking in the warmth like shiny green grapes, with all the pollen floating in the air around them like magic dust. I am in sympathy with it all, I really am. On mating days like today I am especially in sympathy with our dogs, Miss Sadie and Princess. One in heat, the other not. One feeling fullness and tenderness in her loins, damp as the dew, sweet as honeysuckle, and the other just laying against the fence. Then here come the stud dogs, snorting and sweating a thick lather so sour it's like something died.

But a female has to accept this as part of life, she even has to glorify it. Watch my girls listen for the sound of tires on the gravel road. Watch them rise from the couch like a shot, go brush their hair for all it's worth. And if a boy stops his car here and gets out, those girls will be on the porch looking down, smiling with all the pride of Bathsheba. But life being what it is, they know that even beauty will only take them so far. It's far better to have gumption and the courage to live by your wits. Like Rachel, who, being barren, actually trades away her husband for a pile of mandrakes.

It's all here, on page thirty-three of the King James Bible, inspiration and entertainment both, my mating day companion:

And Reuben went in the days of the wheat harvest, and found mandrakes in the field, and brought them unto his mother Leah. Then Rachel said to Leah, Give me, I pray thee, of thy son's mandrakes. And she said unto her, Is it a small matter that thou hast taken my husband? And wouldest thou take away my son's mandrakes also? And Rachel said, Therefore he shall lie with thee tonight for thy son's mandrakes.

I like to think of Leah waiting in the tent, so old by now that she has four grown boys out there in the desert. I like to think of her waiting for Jacob to roll back the canvas to see his old first wife again, smiling, ready. She has won him back, thanks to her firstborn son, who happens to be good at gathering plants out of the field, but not just any plants—mandrakes, which if you read your Bible commentary you will know are plants in the shape of the human body, and they give you the power of your sex. They make you ripe as the wheat, fertile as the field—they give you pregnancy, which is all Rachel ever wanted, isn't it?

So Rachel dreams of mandrakes rising from the ground like little naked madonnas. In the moonlight, the mandrakes rise, so silent and sexy she thinks she can feel them grow. When young

Reuben, handsome and strong, comes walking up with a hand-ful of mandrakes, Rachel will give anything to have them for herself! She'll even give Leah her husband, because she knows the mandrakes will do their trick eventually. (Think of Rachel holding the plants lovingly. Think of how she takes them in the house and rubs them between the palms of her hands, letting the seeds fall, letting the green lifeblood of those roots sink into her skin—she can make herself a sex-inducing pomade.)

The amazing thing is, Rachel finally gets her own baby boy, and he's Joseph—the beautiful one, the good one, the one with the coat of many colors. And it all started with mandrakes. Either that makes perfect sense or it's just nonsense—you choose. On days like today it's plain to me that the world is a great con-suming thing, a huge wonderment of death and desire—all nonsense, mostly. I sit in here with the book of inspiration and Jim stands out back like God, creator of puppies, populating the forest, filling up our yard with life abundant, running wild. And some will live, and some will die. Even Jim can make it happen sometimes, smothering the runts under a sack, snuffing out the crippled ones and the weak—and breathing life into the stillborn, puffing air into the tiny muzzles of the non-breathing. Little pups squirm from death to life right there in his hands.

But life can go like a snap. Train bears down, puppies get in the way. And up high, up on a swivel seat with a panoramic view comes the engineer, eyes looking down the rails. Could he be God? The engineer would stop the train if only it weren't such a massive thing, tons of steel and loads of coal brung up from the pit of the earth, and it comes barreling, burning those rails at lightning speed with the sound of thunder. Leaves on the trees peel back, and the train comes through, making its own wind.

The engineer can hardly stop it. So yes, the puppies die under the weight of that train. Yes, they do die, and their bones—those that aren't crushed by the sharp unforgiving wheels, become food for the earth and sifting sand.

Tonight, when the moonlight fills the windows and the woods are quiet, I'll think of Jacob's ladder, how he lay with his head on a stone and dreamed of angels going up and down. I'll stand in the window while everyone else is asleep and look out and see clouds pass over the moon, just like angels. Then, close to dawn, when the whole sky begins to fill with light, and the moon shines on, and the clouds become gray around the edges, I'll hear the first train of the day, heavy in the distance. You may think I'm crazy but on a night like that, I imagine I'm an angel outside, high in the air, and I swoop down over the train, down in front, a kind of airy, shimmering vapor, and I sweep all living things out from the rails—sweep them to safety. Which is more than Jacob's angels could do. They shall be as dust of the earth, said the God of Abraham, and not long after that, Jacob took his famous trip to the land of Laban and Rachel and Leah, and you know the rest.

But listen, if Jim is God and I am an angel and these puppies are all the created creatures of the earth, then we are definitely in a sad condition. The thing you have to say about the Bible and all the actual stories of God is that everything's a mystery, which is to say it's all nonsense to a limited mind like ours. If God can use a plant in the shape of a human body to help create Joseph, leader of his people, then you know life's a mystery, and there's no sense in trying to touch it. Mating days, we try, we really do. Ask Jim and he'll tell you he's the one in control. But I've got news for him, he's not.

ACKNOWLEDGMENTS

'm profoundly grateful to Hub City Press for choosing this collection of stories for their inaugural C. Michael Curtis Short Story Book Prize. To Betsy Teter, who had the audacity and vision to create such an important small press, thank you. I'm so honored to be counted as one of your authors. And to Kate McMullen and Meg Reid, torchbearers for Hub City Press, thank you for leading me through.

To Lee K. Abbott, thank you, thank you.

And to C. Michael Curtis: For nearly as long as I've been writing, I've looked to you as the sharpest, wisest reader of stories. I hope I measure up, here and there.

Thank you to the journals that first published these stories, in slightly different form: "Submission," the *Alaska Quarterly Review*; "The After-Life," *Narrative*; "Church Retreat, 1975," *Shenandoah*; "Foods of the Bible," *Crazyhorse*; and "Mating Day," *Witness*.

To the Sewanee Writers' Conference, thank you for offering me a place to grow as a writer. In 2014, after working for ten years on a novel about Abraham Lincoln, I finally admitted defeat and returned to the short story. I'll always be grateful to Sewanee for nudging me back into a fruitful, creative life as a story writer. Thank you, Christine Schutt, for assuring me that I had not wasted a decade. Thank you also to the writers in my workshop, especially Monica McFawn, who gave me crazy praise, and to Darrell Nicholson, who allowed me to follow the two of you to the Fiery Gizzard Trail, where I began to imagine a new story.

To the Napa Valley Writers' Conference and Lan Samantha Chang, I learned so much from you. Thank you as well to the Virginia Quarterly Review conference, where I was at last introduced to Bret Anthony Johnston, the best writing teacher I know.

Most recently I'm grateful for the good fortune of attending the Disquiet International Literary Program in Lisbon, an exceptional gathering of artists. To Ru Freeman, thank you. Thank you, too, Deanne Fitzmaurice. You taught me how to see. And to Jose Tereso, street artist and tuk-tuk driver, thank you for the lesson in graffiti, friend. We shall meet again.

The Virginia Center for the Creative Arts, thank you for generous fellowships.

Above all, I am eternally grateful to the Warren Wilson MFA Program for Writers. To Ellen Bryant Voight, thank you for creating such a rigorous and supportive program for writers at work. Thank you to my instructors Susan Neville, Andrea Barrett, Kevin "Mc" McIlvoy, and Claire Messud. An added note of appreciation, Claire, for carrying me through a tough residency just after my mother's passing. You were patient and kind.

To Phyllis Theroux, brilliant essayist and teacher, thank you for helping me get to Warren Wilson in the first place.

To my students at William & Mary thank you for keeping me sharp. My life has been enriched by each of you.

And to my husband, Ed, thank you for hearing every word I write. Your advice is advice I trust.

This book is dedicated to the memory of George Garrett, my dear friend and mentor. After attending a weekend conference in South Carolina many years ago (featuring Mary Oliver, Pattiann Rogers, Judith Kitchen, Richard Bausch and George Garrett—who could stay away?), I joined the legion of young writers brought along by George. So thank you, George, for sneaking me into your MFA fiction workshop so that I could learn, and thank you for including me as an "associate artist" in your workshop at the Atlantic Center for the Arts. Those three weeks meant everything.

Finally, this book is also dedicated to the memory of my mother, who slipped me a small check before each Warren Wilson residency. Knowing she wouldn't last, she slipped me two checks in the end. Thank you for believing.

— C. MICHAEL CURTIS —
SHORT STORY BOOK PRIZE

The C. Michael Curtis Short Story Book Prize includes $10,000 and book publication. The prize is named in honor of C. Michael Curtis, who has served as an editor of *The Atlantic* since 1963 and as fiction editor since 1982. This prize is made possible by an anonymous contribution from a South Carolina donor.

The namesake of the prize, C. Michael Curtis, has discovered or edited Tobias Wolff, Joyce Carol Oates, John Updike, and Anne Beattie, among many others. He has edited several acclaimed anthologies, including *Contemporary New England Stories*, *God: Stories*, and *Faith: Stories*. Curtis moved to Spartanburg, S.C. in 2006 and has taught as a professor at both Wofford and Converse Colleges, in addition to serving on the editorial board of Hub City Press.

RECENT PRIZE WINNERS

Let Me Out Here • Emily W. Pease

HUB CITY PRESS has emerged as the South's premier independent literary press. Focused on finding and spotlighting new and extraordinary voices from the American South, the press has published over eighty high-caliber literary works. Hub City is interested in books with a strong sense of place and is committed to introducing a diverse roster of lesser-heard Southern voices. We are funded by the National Endowment for the Arts, the South Carolina Arts Commission and hundreds of donors across South Carolina.

RECENT HUB CITY PRESS TITLES

What Luck, This Life • Kathryn Schwille

The Wooden King • Thomas McConnell

Whiskey & Ribbons • Leesa Cross-Smith

Bell MT Pro

10.8 / 15.3